Lizzie's Soccer Showdown

John Danakas

James Lorimer & Company, Publishers
Toronto, 1994

James Lorimer & Company Ltd. acknowledges with thanks the support of the Canada Council, the Ontario Arts Council and the Ontario Publishing Centre in the development of writing and publishing in Canada.

Cover illustration: Daniel Shelton

Canadian Cataloguing in Publication Data

Danakas, John
Lizzie's Soccer Showdown

(Sports stories)
ISBN 1-55028-465-7 (bound) ISBN 1-55028-464-9 (pbk.)

I. Title. II. Series: Sports stories (Toronto, Ont.).

PS8557.A53L59 1994   jC813'.54   C94-931898-1
PZ7.D35Li 1994

James Lorimer & Company Ltd., Publishers
35 Britain Street
Toronto, Ontario
M5A 1R7

Printed and bound in Canada

Contents

1

Junior High Blues

As I gaze up at Ms. Bernstein standing at the head of the class, the stack of marked test papers clutched to her chest, I start to worry. Believe me, I don't want that test back. It can only bring trouble.

Ms. Bernstein ruffles the papers with her thumb and shakes her head from side to side, as if she wishes she didn't have to hand these tests back.

"I really expected a lot more from this class," Ms. Bernstein says crossly. She stalks up and down the aisles between desks, handing back the test papers. They fly at us like unwanted pieces of mail. "You're my brightest group of grade sevens, but you have to learn to work a little harder. A class average of 54 per cent is simply unacceptable."

I swap an eye-rolling glance with my best friend Neena Raman and feel my palms sweat and my heart rattle.

I'm hoping Ms. Bernstein doesn't single me out. I like her a lot, but I sure hate it when she makes a fuss over my marks. Right now I'll just take back my test and keep the mark to myself, thank you. I don't need the added embarrassment of the rest of the class gawking at me like I'm some sort of freak of nature.

In the next instant, however, Ms. Bernstein reaches my desk and returns my test. The mark is inscribed in the top right corner in huge red numbers. Then she stops and turns to address the rest of the class.

"As for Lizzie ... " Ms. Bernstein begins. The waft from her perfume fills my nostrils. I can feel the stares from everyone in the classroom boring into me like laser beams.

No, Ms. Bernstein, I hear myself thinking, please, no, don't say anything else, don't hold me up to ridicule, don't torture me this way!

But my prayers go unanswered.

"... well, once again, Lizzie Lucas has shown me what everybody in this class is capable of if you just put in an honest effort. Her test paper was the lone ray of light in a rather bleak overall performance. Congratulations, Lizzie."

That's it, she's done it!

This might be Ms. Bernstein's History class, but right now I'm the one who's history. The rest of the class is going to hate me. I hang my head in shame over my test paper, my nose buried between my folded arms, the bright red 95 per cent staring me right between the eyeballs. I wish there were a secret passageway somewhere under my desk that I could just crawl into and disappear.

Ms. Bernstein moves on, and I'm left alone to the angry glares of my classmates. I sneak a peak over my arm and see them all staring at me. Jasmine Hunt looks like a pit bull ready to attack a slab of raw meat. Victor Pocik is so mad he might as well have steam blowing out his ears.

I crumple up the test paper and stuff it into the knapsack at my feet. I'll find out what I answered wrong when I get home. If I make it there alive.

"Didja have to make us look so bad?" Brad Yee growls from the desk behind mine. I feel a jolt as his right foot kicks the metal basket underneath the seat of my desk.

Brad's what I'd call a "used-to-be" friend. Last year he'd walk home from school with Neena and me, entertaining us with his silly knock-knock jokes. This year he grew three inches, spiked his hair, took to wearing an earring, and acts like he's never known us. Now he's one of the cool crowd, and he holds a grudge against anything or anyone who reminds him of his past.

I wish I could defend myself somehow against these insults, but I hardly ever say a word in class and I'm not about to start now. It's not my fault I do well in school. I like to read — everything from comic books to the encyclopedia — and learning just seems to come naturally to me. I suppose I could try to do worse on the next test, but I'm not willing to go that far just to make everyone else happy.

Frankly, my whole year at Corydon Junior High has been an absolute write-off. Only Neena has stuck by me. She's basically in the same boat I am. Her parents are just as strict as mine — we're never allowed to attend school dances or visit friends past supper time or hang out with the gang at Seven-Eleven. If you're twelve years old like us, that kind of cramps your style, right there.

I know everybody thinks we're real geeks, shy and quiet, with no social life. People think I'm a certified bookworm and Neena is a true-blue goody-goody, but that's not the case at all.

I suppose you could call me shy because I'm usually afraid to speak up, but that doesn't mean I never *want* to say anything. In fact, sometimes I'll spend a whole night thinking about what I *should* have said earlier that day at school, to one of the girls who was being snooty or to one of the guys being rude. What I come up with sounds really good in the middle of the night, too, but I never do get around to saying it face-to-face.

As for Neena, take my word for it, she's no goody-goody. The other students have built a shell around her just because she's kind of different. For example, sometimes she wears her sari to school. In most students' eyes, that makes Neena a dweeb. But, believe me, Neena knows how to have a good time. There's always a twinkle in her eye, and she comes up with great ideas for things for the two of us to do. Sometimes I think that if she were ever allowed some breathing space, look out! She could be the life of any party.

It's just not fair.

Ms. Bernstein by now has finished handing back the tests and is writing out the correct answers on the chalkboard. Most of the eyes in the classroom slowly peel off me and turn to the front.

"Way to go, Lizzie," Neena whispers to me now, smiling and winking an eye at me. "I'm really proud of you."

That makes me feel a little better. I like the way Neena always seems to know just what to say. I guess that's what friendship is all about.

"How'd you do?" I ask Neena.

Neena cups her hands over her mouth and moves her lips silently. I make out a seventy-nine, which I think is really good, and give her the thumbs-up sign.

Neena brightens, and right away I'm reminded of how beautiful she is, even though the rest of the class hasn't seemed to notice. Her skin's dark, the colour of fresh coffee beans, and she has long, frizzy black hair down past her shoulders and the most astonishing eyes I have ever seen, kind of blue and black at the same time, like sapphires (which I've actually seen and touched at Neena's father's jewelry store in Portage Place downtown). She's not a conventional beauty, but when you spot her in a crowd you can't help taking a long look at her, which is exactly what people mean, I guess, when they say someone is "striking."

I'm afraid I can't say the same for myself. I'm what people mean when they say someone is "gangling." I'm taller than most girls in my class, but I'm kind of skinny, with little shape to speak of. I also wear braces (happily, which you'd understand if you saw the awful shape my teeth are in), and my hair — straight and mid-length — is brown. So are my eyes. Unfortunately, most people do not classify brown as one of the more thrilling colours.

Neena is East Indian, and I'm Greek. I mean, we were both born in Canada, but our parents are from those countries. You'd think that because our parents are from different parts of the world, we'd be kind of different, but actually it makes us kind of the same. In fact, we're always finding things about ourselves and our families that we have in common. For example, until last year we both had to spend two nights a week taking classes, which we detested, in our parents' native languages. You could say we're the same in the way we're different — if that makes any sense.

Ms. Bernstein begins writing out the names of the last five prime ministers, which was probably the toughest question on the test. I see Frank Miller slap his forehead with the palm of his hand as the name Pierre Elliot Trudeau wriggles across the board, and Jasmine rifles through her textbook to double-check something, as if she believes Ms. Bernstein has made some sort of mistake. That's Jasmine for you, always working overtime to earn extra marks. She's the same way about being popular, always trying hard to cozy up to the in crowd, laughing at all the right jokes, making fun of all the right people. It works for her, but I know I could never be like that.

To tell the truth, I'm kind of bored right now. I answered most of these questions correctly, remember, so I need something else to do. I tear out a sheet of paper from my binder and turn to Neena. She's always game.

"Want to play Hollywood?" I whisper.

Neena looks as bored as I do. "Sure," she whispers back. "You start."

Hollywood's a game we play that's kind of like *Wheel of Fortune* on TV (except we don't give away the fabulous prizes!). It's a lot of fun. One of us thinks of a movie title and draws a series of blank lines across the page, one blank line for every letter in the movie title. The other person guesses one letter at a time, trying to figure out the title. We've been playing Hollywood all year and still haven't been caught, which I think is kind of funny because everybody seems to think we just sit in our desks dully and listen to every word that comes out of the teacher's mouth.

Before we know it, the buzzer goes off and class is finally over.

In one swift motion, I grab my knapsack and push myself out of my desk.

"Hold on, everybody," Ms. Bernstein shouts then. "I've been asked by Coach Borowski and Coach Laughton to make an announcement."

Everybody in the class is standing by their desks, books in hand, feet pointed to the side door, eyes staring at the clock, waiting for Ms. Bernstein to complete her announcement.

"Soccer tryouts begin today for both the boys' team and the girls' team. The boys will practise at the near field and the girls at the far, at four o'clock sharp. All boys or girls interested in joining their respective teams should make sure to attend."

Unlike some of the boys, who greet this piece of information with obvious excitement, I couldn't care less. I'm just waiting for a cue to take off.

Ms. Bernstein looks up from her notes. "Thank you. You may leave now."

The class stampedes to the door.

Before I know it, I'm squished between three or four burly guys and I don't think it's my imagination that I feel them putting a little extra pressure into their shoulders as they squeeze by me. By the time I'm through the door I figure I'll resemble a pretzel.

When I'm finally safely outside, I rush to the locker I share with Neena and take out my trumpet for Music class.

Our locker is plastered with posters of TV and movie hunks and gorgeous women — more than necessary if you ask me — but I think Neena is trying to make up for the fact that her parents don't allow her to hang any posters in her bedroom.

From the locker three slots down from ours, Kayla Delmonte — the class beauty queen — sends a series of dirty looks our way, probably meant to show her rather general dissatisfaction over our recent behaviour in class.

"This is getting ridiculous," I say. "You and I are public enemy number one and number two around here."

"I know," Neena says. "We can't win for losing. What does a girl have to do to earn some popularity in this crummy school?"

"Beats me." I slam our locker shut with a loud clang and wheel around to head to the next class.

But I stop dead in my tracks.

Justin Hope, the most popular boy of all the grade sevens (because he's not only gorgeous but also quite a nice guy; not that he's ever spoken more than a few words to me), has just appeared beside us. His locker just happens to be right next to ours. Well, if truth be told, that was no accident: Neena made sure our locker was situated as close as possible to Justin's by cutting in line right behind him when it was time to pick up locker numbers. Whenever Justin shows up, with his long blond hair tied in a ponytail and those cute blue eyes, Neena and I linger around a little. You never know, one day he may actually have a whole conversation with us.

"Are you trying out for the soccer team?" he asks now.

Of course, the question is not directed to Neena and me, but to Kayla.

"I don't think so," Kayla replies. "Soccer's not my sport."

She bats her eyelashes at Justin. I think she's trying to tell Justin her favourite sport is more along the lines of romance, but he doesn't get the message. Boys can be thick that way sometimes.

"That's too bad." Justin hangs up his Toronto Raptors jacket and takes out his books. He starts walking to his next class and Kayla steps alongside him. "I love soccer."

That's all Neena needs to hear. As soon as Justin and Kayla are out of earshot, her mouth races into maximum overdrive.

"What would you say, Lizzie, to you and me trying out for the soccer team?" she asks breathlessly.

"I'd say my best friend has finally gone la-la. I've got Music class right now, and you've got French. Let's get going."

"No, I'm serious," she continues. I take a good look at her and swear I can actually see the wheels turning inside her head. "Just imagine: we make the team, help the girls win the championship, and the whole school, including Justin Hope, loves us. The girls' soccer team is our ticket to popularity. Can't you just see it?"

One of Neena's biggest problems, I must say, is her over-active imagination.

"No, I can't see it." I hate to rain on Neena's parade but sometimes it's best to be straight with the ones you love, if you know what I mean.

"Really?" She seems shocked that I don't share her excitement.

"Really," I go on, explaining myself. "You know what I see, Neena? I see you and me making absolute fools of ourselves out on the soccer field and the rest of the girls on the team sharing one big laugh at our expense. I see a lifetime of unpopularity in front of us worse than anything we've endured up to now. Soccer's out of the question."

"Hold on, Lizzie, hold on." Neena nabs me by the shoulder. "Don't you always say you love playing soccer?"

"Yeah," I admit. I play with my family all the time and consider soccer my favourite sport. I tilt my nose in the air jokingly. "And if I may say so, I'm very good at it." Then I scrunch up my face and stare at Neena. "But so what?"

"So what? So you teach me everything you know and we'll have no trouble making the team."

"You've been reading too many fairy tales to your little brother," I say. "Real life's not so rosy, sweetheart."

The hallway is emptying out and a quick glance at the clock tells me we have about thirty seconds to get to the next class.

"Oh no!" I cry out. "Let's hurry."

We're half-jogging down the hallway. My trumpet case is banging against my thigh. Lizzie's French text is slapping against her chest.

"Just trust me on this one, will you?" Neena begs. "You're my best friend."

I can't help cracking a smile. I owe Neena more favours than I can even remember.

"OK, I give in," I say. "Only because we're best friends."

"I knew you'd come around." Neena's eyes sparkle. "We'll make a big splash on that girls' soccer team, you'll see."

That's exactly what I'm afraid of, I think to myself, making a big splash. Something along the lines of a belly flop.

I make a bee-line down the hallway towards Music class. Neena swerves towards French class.

The buzzer rings and I feel its noise humming through every bone in my body. I'm late.

We finally make the decision to do something about our images, and I'm already in trouble.

"Meet you by the girls' washroom at four," Neena calls out to me.

"Our futures are in your hands," I answer back.

2

Soccer, Anyone?

After school, Neena and I meet in the girls' washroom at the far end of the school to change into our gym clothes. Then, while another girl stands two centimetres from the mirror applying makeup to her face, Neena pulls her hair back into a tight bun and I tuck in my T-shirt.

"I'll just follow your leads out on the field," Neena says.

"OK," I say, but I know our little scheme is far from OK. I tell myself not to think too much about what we're about to do because if I do, I know I won't dare go through with it.

The truth is the only soccer I've played is with my family, during picnics at the beach. We usually play the boys (my dad and my brother Perry) against the girls (my mother, my sister Sia, and me). We have a lot of fun, and sometimes, when my mom's wearing the right shoes, we girls even beat the boys. Of course, it's all very casual, and I get the idea my father doesn't always try his hardest. In fact, I know he doesn't, because he's really quite good. Back in Greece, he played two seasons with a third-division team called Ilisiakos. He's got a picture of the team hanging in his office at work. All the players are bunched together in two neat rows, and he's the guy kneeling up front with the ball trapped under his hand. When he plays with us, I'm sure he holds back, but not so much that it's obvious. I actually enjoy our family soccer games.

The question is, will I enjoy playing on the school team?

As Neena and I make our way onto the soccer field, I feel awfully self-conscious. Neena's body has already developed and she looks fantastic in shorts and a T-shirt (although, like me, she always complains that her arms are too hairy). Beside her, I'm sure I resemble something along the lines of a flag-pole. I notice that some of the boys on the near field have turned and are watching Neena, probably trying to figure out, from that distance, who she is. As to my identity, I'm sure none of them are in the least bit curious, if in fact they've even spotted me.

Coach Laughton is standing by the goalposts at the far field, and there are only three girls around her, lazily kicking a soccer ball back and forth. I can't make out their faces. The sun is hot, and Coach Laughton is wiping sweat from her brow. She's wearing a metal whistle around her neck and looks all business.

"I wonder if we're early," I comment to Neena.

"Yeah," Neena says, "you'd think there'd be more girls out."

The school soccer fields have just been mowed and you can smell the cut grass heavy in the air. I sneeze. Must be my allergies acting up again.

As we reach the practice area, I see Coach Laughton look worriedly at her watch and shake her head from side to side. Meanwhile, the three girls nod, but they don't say hello. One of the girls is Jasmine Hunt and she makes a face — her eyes all screwed up and her lower lip pushed far out — like Neena and I are the last two girls she'd expect to see at the soccer tryout. The other two girls are Natalie Lundstrom and Melanie Kline.

Natalie is one of the nicest girls in the cool crowd. She says hi to everybody she meets in the hallway and will always listen to whatever you have to say. I think she has more best friends than anyone else in grade seven.

Melanie is a whole other story. I don't know too much about her except that her older brother committed suicide two years ago. Everybody in our neighbourhood knows about that. Ever since then Melanie has kept pretty much to herself, saying very little and spending most of her time clued out from the rest of the world, listening to music on her Walkman. She does go out for all the school sports, though, and she's usually one of the best players.

I take a closer look at Coach Laughton. I've heard she's almost fifty years old, but she looks way younger than that, even though she wears no makeup at all and her blonde hair is going grey at the roots. Her body is trim and tanned, and her smile's wide and white. In gym class she often tells us about the mountains she climbs and the trails she hikes over summer vacation.

"Did you see any other girls on their way to this practice?" Coach Laughton asks us when we report to her. "It's already ten minutes past four."

"No," Neena says, and points with her chin to the other three girls gathered around the goalpost. "I guess we're it."

Coach Laughton shades her eyes with her hand as if she's saluting someone and gazes back at the school doors. But there's nobody there.

"We just don't have enough girls," she says finally, shrugging her shoulders.

"What does that mean?" Natalie asks.

"I'm afraid," Coach Laughton replies, "that means there won't be a girls' soccer team this year at Corydon Junior High School."

"You've got to be kidding!" Natalie cries out.

"That can't be!" Jasmine whines.

I can tell Melanie is upset as well. She kicks the dirt around the goalpost with the toe of her cleat. Her upper legs are ridged with muscle, like a chiselled piece of wood.

"I'm not kidding," Coach Laughton says. She holds her hands out in the air, palms up. "Five girls do not make up a soccer team. There's nothing we can do."

"But I really want to play soccer!" Natalie goes on.

"So do I!" Jasmine echoes.

"Me too!" pouts Neena.

Good for her, I think. She's really into this.

Melanie simply kicks at the dirt again.

Of course, I stay silent. Who'd listen to me anyhow, even if I did have something to say?

Coach Laughton bends down and grabs the soccer ball from Melanie's feet. "I guess that's it for our tryout, girls," she says. "Maybe next year you'll have enough girls for a team." Then she begins to gather some other equipment she'd brought with her to the practice, like coloured tops and bright orange plastic pylons. "Come on, girls, give me a hand with these things and let's get going."

"This stinks!" Jasmine gripes. She marches away towards the school.

"We might as well kiss goodbye my great idea for impressing Justin and maybe earning some popularity around here," Neena sighs as she helps Melanie and me pick up the remaining equipment.

"You know what?" I toss a soccer ball up into the air and bounce it off my head a few times, a trick my father taught me. "I really wanted this to work out."

"I guess it's back to the drawing board for us."

Neena and I follow Coach Laughton and the other girls off the field. Our heads are drooped down, and nobody says a word. The sunshine is like a weight on my shoulders. I kind of wish some dark clouds would gather in the sky to match my mood.

As we pass the boys practising at the near field, all five of us stop to watch them. They have a full turnout of players, all right, and then some. Right now the boys are in pairs passing the ball to each other. Some of them are really good and kick the ball hard while still managing to keep it in a straight line to their partner. Coach Borowski is moving from pair to pair, telling the players what they're doing wrong, patting them on the back when they do well. The whole practice seems to be running like clockwork.

"Aren't they lucky!" Jasmine jeers.

"Now, now," Coach Laughton breaks in. "It's not the boys' fault that we didn't get enough girls out for a team."

"I know," Natalie comments. "But the boys do always seem to have it made when it comes to school sports."

"Come on, girls," Coach Laughton says, "let's call it an afternoon."

We start walking, Coach Laughton up ahead, then Natalie and Jasmine, then Melanie, and then Neena and I.

But Neena is stalling. Her eyes linger on the pleasant sight of Justin straining his leg to push a pass directly to his partner. I let my mind wonder for a few silly seconds what it would be like to play soccer with these boys.

And then, all of a sudden and for no apparent reason, I can't control myself, yes, me, shy and quiet and awkward little Lizzie Lucas, the bookworm who never so much as makes a peep, who is afraid to string two words together in public without thinking long and hard over them, I open my big mouth, open it up wide, and — without thinking, without planning, just spurting out exactly what I feel — say: "Why don't we just join the boys' team?"

It's like lightning struck. Coach Laughton and the girls, Neena included, make a sudden one-eighty degree turn and stare at me bug-eyed. I don't think they can believe what I've just said, or even that I've said anything at all. So I say it again.

"Why don't we just join the boys' team?" I'm looking straight at Coach Laughton. My eyes peer into hers. My heart's beating so fast I can feel it like a motor inside my chest.

"Think about it," I go on. "What's stopping us from just crossing over to the far field and joining the boys' practice? We want to play soccer, and they're playing soccer, so why don't we play together?"

Coach Laughton is still silent. She has a totally blank look on her face, like my logic is maybe just a little illogical.

"Yeah," Neena pipes in. "That makes perfect sense."

I knew she'd back me up.

Natalie and Jasmine have moved in behind me. Natalie pats me on the shoulder. "I like Lizzie's idea," she says. I turn to look at her and she smiles at me warmly.

Coach Laughton bites her lower lip and squints her eyes. I can tell she's thinking. Hard.

"Let me get this straight, Lizzie," she says. "You want to go over to the boys' practice and tell them the girls want to join them. Is that right?"

I stand tall, push out my chest.

"Exactly."

"And then what?" Coach Laughton asks.

"And then we all play soccer together," I answer. "That's what we all want — boys and girls — isn't it, to play soccer?" They're not saying anything, but somehow I can feel the other girls supporting me, pushing me on. I don't think I've talked so much all year long to anybody at school but Neena. I have to admit, it feels great.

"And you think this is going to work, that the boys will like this idea?"

"It's worth trying."

I don't know why, but I look at Melanie then. It's like I want to know what she has to say about my idea.

To my surprise, I get a response. Melanie's eyes are burning intensely.

"It's worth trying," she repeats in a monotone.

All together the rest of the girls shout, "Yeah!"

Jasmine breaks away from the other girls for a moment and takes a long, hard look at me, like she's trying to figure something out. "I never would have expected this to be your idea," she says. "Maybe you're all right, Lizzie."

Yeah, maybe I am, I think.

"OK," Coach Laughton says, a smile tickling the corners of her mouth. "There might be some school board regulations against this sort of thing, but I suppose we can deal with that later. Let's go, girls."

We all start marching in unison behind Coach Laughton towards the boys' soccer practice.

"This should be exciting," I gasp to Neena.

"No kidding," Neena says. "Beats going home after school and watching old reruns on TV. I can't believe this was all your idea."

"Neither can I," I say. Suddenly, my throat goes dry and the inside of my stomach starts twirling like a baton. "Does this mean I get all the blame if we fall flat on our faces?"

Neena smiles. "Yeah, best friend, that's exactly what it means. I suggested we play soccer, but on the girls' team. This business about trying out for the boys' team is your bright idea."

"I'm scared," I say.

"So am I," Neena admits. Her sapphire eyes flicker. "But sometimes it's fun to be scared."

Going by the strange but curiously enjoyable feeling in my stomach right now, I'd say she's right.

3

Making a Case

Coach Borowski notices us approaching the boys' practice field out of the corner of his eye. With a wave of his right hand, he motions to the boys to continue with their drills and then he starts to walk over to us. He pats his short hair down with the palm of his hand and fixes his jersey.

"Good afternoon, girls, Coach Laughton," he says. I notice the beginning of a smirk sneaking across his mouth. "Come to watch some real soccer, have you?" I can tell he's joking.

"As a matter of fact, Coach Borowski, we're here on official business," Coach Laughton states. She's holding herself straight and hard. I know she's behind us girls all the way. "We have something of a proposal to offer you and your players."

I don't think Coach Borowski has even heard her. He's turned to watch his players and claps his hands enthusiastically as he witnesses Justin drill a perfect half-volley shot into the upper right corner of the net.

"I have a mighty fine group of boys this year," he exclaims. "With a little work, we could go all the way, win the school division championship." He pulls his sweat pants over his waist to cover his round belly. "You were saying, Coach Laughton?"

"I was saying," Coach Laughton continues, just a hint of an edge in her voice, "that we have a proposal to offer you, which I think you'll find very interesting."

I think she has Coach Borowski's attention now. His eyebrows have lifted and his head is tilted forward. "I'm all ears," he says.

"Well, as you can probably see," Coach Laughton holds her hands up towards me and the other girls, "we haven't got enough players this year to form our own soccer team."

"I'm sorry to hear that," Coach Borowski interrupts her. "But how can I help?"

"Quite simply," Coach Laughton continues. "These girls would like to join your team."

Coach Borowski's jaw drops. His eyes squint forward. He looks like he's just seen a UFO.

"Say that again."

"These five girls really want to play soccer this year, so they've decided that they'd like to try out for your team."

"But our team is the boys' team," Coach Borowski says, somehow regaining enough composure to put together a coherent sentence. "And it's called that for a reason, because all the players on it are boys."

"Come on now, Coach Borowski, these are the nineties. If these girls want to play on the boys' team, they should be allowed that opportunity."

"Yeah," Jasmine cries out. "Equal opportunity regardless of race or sex."

"But there are regulations, rules," Coach Borowski insists. His face is turning purple. "What if one of the girls were to get hurt?"

"Are you trying to tell us that no boys ever get hurt playing soccer?" Natalie steps forward and asks, her arms crossed, her lips drawn tight over her teeth.

These girls are not going to be easy to mess with, I realize. Good for them.

"Of course not, but ..." Coach Borowski is stumbling around for the right words. He's looking back at his players for some sort of support. "... but that's different."

"How?" Natalie asks.

All Coach Borowski can muster as a reply is a blank look on his face.

"I think you have to agree, Coach Borowski," Coach Laughton cuts in, "that the girls deserve a chance. At least let them try out for the team."

Coach Borowski fingers the plastic whistle around his neck and thinks a moment. He takes a long look at all of us girls, like he's trying to figure out if we really have it in us to play soccer, and then he takes another long look at the boys. When he finally opens his mouth to speak, I can tell he's being careful, measuring his words, making sure we understand everything he's saying.

"I suppose there's no harm in letting these young ladies try out. Of course, you do realize, Coach Laughton, that there are no guarantees they'll make the team. They'll have to be judged fairly, on an even par with the boys, over the next few practices."

"Of course," Coach Laughton offers. "And I'm sure Melanie, Natalie, Jasmine, Neena and Lizzie wouldn't want it any other way."

Coach Borowski looks right into our eyes then, one girl after the other. "Are you young ladies serious about this? I mean, this isn't just some stunt you're pulling to make a point, is it? You *do* really want to play soccer?"

We all nod our heads in agreement.

"And you don't want any special privileges, just the chance to try out for the team, fair and square and on equal footing with the boys?"

"That's right," Natalie answers.

"Well," Coach Borowski says, "let it never be said that I stopped someone who really wanted to play soccer. It's the best sport there is." He pushes out his hand and shakes Coach Laughton's. "Your girls are welcome to our tryouts. Follow me."

We pat one another on the back, and Coach Laughton winks and gives us the A-OK sign. I have the uncomfortable feeling that Coach Borowski is only letting us try out for the boys' team because he thinks we probably won't make it, but I don't say anything. I figure it's best to give him the benefit of the doubt. Besides, if he is thinking we can't cut it, maybe we can prove him wrong.

By now the boys have spotted us walking onto their field, and they stop their practice. Coach Borowski blows his whistle to gather them around him.

"Listen up, boys," he announces as his players flop down onto the grass to rest. "Coach Laughton has something to tell us."

Coach Laughton moves forward. "We have something to ask you boys, and I hope you have open minds about it, because it's kind of important to these five girls here."

"Go ahead," Coach Borowski urges her on.

The boys gawk at us, like we're on display in a zoo. They have no idea why we're standing in the middle of their practice field.

All of a sudden I feel terribly self-conscious and wish that I hadn't opened my mouth a few minutes ago. I slowly ease my way behind Neena so as few of the boys as possible can see me.

That's better, I think to myself. I'm back outside the picture, where I belong.

But not for long.

"Actually," Coach Laughton says, "why don't I let the girl who had this idea make the announcement? She's the one who deserves the credit, and maybe you boys will be more accepting of the proposal if it comes from one of your fellow students and not from one of the teaching staff."

Please, I don't need that kind of favour.

But Coach Laughton turns her head around to find me. By then, of course, I've disappeared behind Neena.

"Lizzie?" she calls out. "Lizzie?"

Then she spots me burrowing myself into an imaginary hole.

"Lizzie," she says, "why don't you come up here and tell these boys about your idea?"

I hesitate, but then Neena takes a few steps to the side to let me through and nudges me with her elbow.

"Come on," Neena urges, "if this were my idea I'd be shouting it from the top of the goalposts."

I plod my way forward and face the boys. They're all eyeing me with curiosity, waiting for me to say something. I feel ten times worse than I did first term when I had to deliver an oral report in front of the class for my science project. Electromagnetic fields were a lot easier to talk about than the news I have to break now to the boys.

All of a sudden I'm not so brave.

"Well," I begin, looking down at my sneakers, as if I'm speaking to them and not the boys, "there aren't enough girls to make up our own soccer team so ..."

"So what?" one of the boys cries out.

"... so we'd like to join yours," I finish my sentence, meekly, as if I'm not so much stating our intention as tossing off a silly idea.

"You've got to be kidding!"

"You must be nuts!"

"No way!"

"This is a *boys'* team!"

The shouts from the boys come at me like so many stones thrown at my face. I don't know who says what because my eyes are still on my sneakers. But something inside tells me to fight back. This is ridiculous. The boys should at least hear us out. I'm like a steaming kettle ready to blow its top.

I hold up my head and raise my voice as loud as I can.

"We just want a chance to try out for the team!" My nerve is definitely back. In fact, right now I'm all nerves.

In retaliation, the boys pipe up.

"Who are *you,* anyhow?" Tyler McNaught yells.

"Aren't you that bookworm who's always making the rest of the class look bad?" Victor hollers.

"Since when did they let geeks talk?" Brad barks.

I'm about as close to crying now as you can get without tears falling from your eyes. But I don't cry. No way. I wouldn't give Brad and the other boys the pleasure.

Coach Borowski waves his hands in front of himself to silence the boys.

"Take it easy, boys," he says. "Take it easy." I can tell he's not too happy with their reaction. "This isn't the end of the world. These girls are keen on playing soccer, so, considering they don't have a team of their own, I think we owe them the favour of letting them practise with us."

He looks directly at Brad. "It's the *sportsmanlike* thing to do. At least until we come up with some other solution."

Then he sneaks a concerned look at Coach Laughton and continues. "For all I know, this could be against the school board regulations. We'll have to check with Principal Murray on that. But in the meantime I think we should cooperate and make these girls feel at home on our practice field. How's that?" He has a stern set to his eyes. Thin lines of sweat are trickling down his face.

"So this isn't a permanent arrangement?" Victor asks.

"Not necessarily," Coach Borowski answers. "We'll just have to wait and see what happens. But that shouldn't matter to you. Let's not forget why we're out here — to play soccer. And nobody's stopping us from doing that. So, as far as I can see, there's nothing to complain about."

"Come on, guys," Justin calls out. His voice has "team leader" written all over it. "We're missing something on this team. Who knows? Maybe these girls'll help us find it."

"Yeah," Frank Miller adds, "what's the big deal? If we think we're so good, why should we be afraid to let these girls try out for our team? Is anybody afraid they might lose their position to a girl?"

The boys start to talk among themselves. We can't hear what they're saying but it's obvious that they're lightening up. They even break into laughter once or twice. By the looks and sounds of it, they're starting to think this is one big joke. I'm sure they believe there's no way we'll get permission to play on the boys' team.

"What'll they do when it's time to play shirts against skins?" one boy jibes.

"Does this mean we have to change in the same locker room?" another boy scoffs.

I do my best to ignore their taunts, but it's not easy. Neena and I wanted to play soccer in order to make friends, not to create more enemies.

Finally, Justin stands up and approaches me. He puts out his hand, and it takes me a few seconds to figure out that he's waiting for me to shake hands with him. I stretch out my hand and we shake. His handshake is warm and confident.

"Welcome to our first practice," he says. "Good luck."

As far as I can tell, he's sincere.

"Thank you," I say.

We've just made ourselves a deal. For the time being at least, the girls will be playing on the boys' soccer team.

Justin and the other boys rise and move back onto the practice field.

"Way to go, Liz!" Natalie raves. "Thanks to you, we just might get to play soccer this year."

"And on the boys' team!" Jasmine enthuses. "This is exciting!"

Coach Laughton approaches Coach Borowski then.

"I guess it's your practice now from here on," she says to him. "I trust you'll treat the girls fairly."

"You have my word," Coach Borowski says. "And I'll meet you in Mr. Murray's office sometime tomorrow so we can straighten this all out before the next practice."

"It's a deal," Coach Laughton says. She nods at us girls then. "I know you'll do well, girls. I'd stay to root you on but this is Coach Borowski's team and I don't want to get in his way. We have to do this right, if you know what I mean."

I think I do. If we girls are going to make the boys' soccer team, we're going to have to do everything by the book. No stepping on anyone's toes, no making unnecessary trouble. It'll be trouble enough just getting Coach Borowski and the boys to give us an honest shot.

"You were great," Neena tells me. We trot behind Coach Borowski to a canvas bag full of soccer balls. "The rest of the girls are really impressed."

"But how about the boys?" I ask.

"I guess you'll have to impress them on the soccer field," Neena replies.

4

Not the Real Thing

W atch this!" Brad announces as the girls position themselves on the field alongside the boys and Coach
Borowski strolls over to the equipment bag to retrieve more
balls.

Brad struts to a ball. The other boys look on, providing
him with an enthusiastic audience. We girls start kicking a
ball to one another, but we can't help keeping one eye on
Brad.

Brad pokes his right foot under the ball and lifts it gently
into the air. Then he bounces the ball with the other foot. He's
being a hot-dog, trying to show just how superior the boys'
skills are by juggling the ball the way I've seen my dad do a
few times. Unfortunately for him, the ball drops to the ground
after only three bounces.

"Let me try that again," Brad says. I can tell his face is
starting to turn pink.

"Keep dreaming!" Jasmine razzes as Brad once again
scoops the ball up with the toe of his right cleat.

Brad dismisses Jasmine with a wave of his hand and
bounces the ball back into the air with his knee. The ball
bounces high but then he can't seem to decide which body
part to use to keep the ball up. He finally lets the ball fall back
to his feet but fails to tap it back up in the air just right. The

ball flies away from him and he goes chasing after it, red and embarrassed.

Jasmine and Natalie laugh heartily. Even some of the boys start ribbing Brad. Serves him right, I think. Lately, he's always trying to make other people laughingstocks. Maybe it's time he got a taste of his own medicine.

But his embarrassment's not over. Melanie moves to the same ball and chips it into the air. Her eyes take on this strange glow, like she's concentrating so hard she sees only the ball and her feet. The ball bounces from one foot to the other. And then from one knee to the other. Then up to her head and into the air and back down to her right foot. Ankles, shoulders, and chest all come into play. Melanie juggles the ball without letting it touch the ground for at least a dozen bounces.

As she passes the ball back to Brad, I see a trace of a smile on her face. She's made her point. Anything a boy can do, a girl can do too, and sometimes better.

Coach Borowski had returned with the extra soccer balls before Melanie's juggling performance was over. Now he nods his head. "Nice control, young lady," he says. "Hope you can use those skills in a game."

The boys exchange silent looks. I wink at Melanie.

We get on with the practice, which turns out to include only the most basic drills. Coach Borowski, you see, obviously just wants to wrap things up, go home, and see what Mr. Murray will have to say tomorrow about the girls playing on the boys' soccer team.

I get the uneasy feeling that this is just a pretend practice.

Other than Brad with his self-inflicted goof-up, Neena's probably the only player on the field who has any trouble with these drills. Soccer's entirely unfamiliar ground for her. She spends most of her time just trying to line up the ball in front of her so she can connect her foot with it cleanly. Sometimes she looks at the ball as if it's just occurred to her today that you can actually set it into motion by striking it with your foot. No question about it, she'll need a lot of work.

Her most embarrassing moment occurs near the end of the practice. We're taking shots on net and finally it's Neena's turn. She takes a running start like she's meaning to wallop the ball with all she's got. But as her foot approaches the ball, she loses her balance. Her feet and the ball get tangled up. Somehow the ball rolls under her foot and she slides over it, like a comedian slipping on a banana peel. She falls knees-first into a patch of hard mud. Her white shorts are dusty with dirt. She closes her eyes hard and waits for the insults to come flying.

But before any of the boys has a chance to say anything smart, Justin springs out from his place in line behind Neena and helps her up by offering his right hand to her. When she's back on her feet, he trots back into line and proceeds to carry out a perfect shot.

He may be wearing shorts and a T-shirt, but to Neena's eyes just then I'm sure Justin looks like a knight in shining armour.

"Now you know what it feels like to hold Justin Hope's hand," I whisper to Neena as I approach her, reminding her that I've already been honoured with that privilege when he shook my hand to welcome us onto the team.

"Do I ever!" Neena exclaims. I can't be sure but I think I see stars in her eyes. "Do you think he was just being a gentleman or that he really likes me?"

"You never know," I say. "I wouldn't hold my breath, though."

I'm not being mean. I just don't want Neena to get her hopes up too high. Besides, right now I figure we have more important things to think about. Like soccer.

The final drill of the practice happens to be my specialty: heading. I figure this'll be as good a chance as any to display my skills. A lot of kids my age are afraid to head the ball. Not me. Dad taught me the proper technique. I keep my eyes wide open, make contact with the centre of my forehead, and push out with my neck and shoulders in the direction I want the ball to travel. Of course, I'm sure it helps matters that I'm quite tall and that my head is exceptionally hard.

During the heading drill, Coach Borowski pairs me up with Enzo Milano. That's fine with me. Enzo, who has brown curly hair and big round eyes, is a pretty good kid. He lives on my block. I end up seeing him a lot over the summer because our dads both keep a vegetable garden alongside the train tracks behind Lindsay Street, and Enzo and I always have to help them with something, like hauling water or picking corn. His dad speaks almost no English, but he somehow manages to communicate his gardening tips (Enzo's dad is *the* master gardener of the neighbourhood) to my dad.

Now, Enzo tosses the ball into the air and moves under it to head it to me. The ball soars high, but I wait it out and push my head into it, passing it back to Enzo, so that the ball ends its arc right above his head.

Enzo meets the ball again, but this time he makes contact mostly with the side of his head. The ball falls directly to the ground.

"Sorry," he says. "I should have had that one. You passed it to me perfectly."

"It's all right," I say. "I'm sure you'll get the hang of it."

Maybe not all the boys are poor sports, I think. At least, Enzo and Justin don't seem to have a problem sharing their team with five girls.

Suddenly, I realize, I'm really getting comfortable out on the field and I wish Coach Borowski would call a scrimmage game or at least allow us to take some practice shots. I could use some real action.

But of course that doesn't happen. Coach Borowski wants to get this practice over with as soon as possible. About a half hour into the practice he blasts his whistle two times and gathers the whole team around him at centre field.

"That's it!" he announces. "Let's call it a day."

"But Coach," Victor shouts, a mischievous grin pasted on his face, "you promised us we could choose our captain today."

"Under the circumstances, Victor," Coach responds sternly, "I think the selection of our captain can wait until next practice."

"Why?" Brad comes to Victor's support. "I say we choose our captain this week."

He whispers something to the boy next to him, who passes the message along to the next boy, until all the boys are in on the secret and sharing Victor's devilish grin.

One after the other, they start pleading with Coach Borowski to allow them to select a captain right then and there, even though this is their first practice!

"OK, OK," Coach Borowski finally succumbs to the request, "if you guys insist."

I think he's making a mistake, but I guess he'll do anything right now to end this practice with as little conflict as possible.

I don't know what the boys are up to, but it sure doesn't smell good to me.

"I'm open to nominations," Coach mumbles.

Brad puts up his hand. He can hardly speak for trying to stifle his laughter.

"I nominate Lizzie Lucas," he says. "That is, if she's still on the team next week." The giggles are let loose from his mouth like pop that squirts up and out your nose when you laugh too hard.

I should have known.

Victor puts up his hand. "I second the nomination."

Several of the boys howl with laughter. I guess I'm the big joke of the day. They figure they'll elect me team captain as a lark, since they figure by next week Mr. Murray will have set us girls straight.

Coach Borowski shakes his head sadly. "Are there any other nominations?" he asks.

I look around. Nobody puts up their hand. The girls look at me with "I wish there was something we could do" expressions on their faces. Victor and Brad are practically rolling on the grass in gleeful appreciation of their little joke.

"Well, then," Coach Borowski informs the team, "it looks like Lizzie Lucas will be our team captain this year." He steps towards me and shakes my hand. I look into his eyes and can tell he's ashamed of his players. "Congratulations, Lizzie," he says. "I'm sure you'll be a fine captain." The funny thing is, I get the feeling he means it.

The boys enjoy one last long laugh at my expense.

I sit there on the grass, feeling dazed. This was not supposed to happen. Who knows what these boys might pull next? Who knows if the girls will even be allowed to continue playing on the boys' team?

Maybe finding out the answers to questions like that just isn't worth the hassle. Maybe I'd be better off crawling back into my shell. All of a sudden, I wish that I'd kept my big mouth shut earlier in the day.

Because now I'm captain of a soccer team that doesn't even want me.

5

What's a Team Captain to Do?

At home that evening over dinner, I feel like telling everybody about my problem, but I can't get a word in. Sia and Perry are waging World War III over who gets to use Mom's car Saturday night. Dad's car, a brand new Monte Carlo, is strictly off limits.

"Mom," pleads Perry, "I've got a date with Cheryl. We're going to a movie and then out for pizza. You can't expect us to take the *bus*, can you?"

Perry says "bus" with the same expression on his face that a baby uses to communicate its attitude toward the taste of cod-liver oil. Ever since he got his hands on a driver's licence last month, he assumes ownership of Mom's car reverts to him in the evenings. He's allowed to go on one date a week and I guess he likes to make the most of it.

"And why can't you take the bus?" Sia cuts in. She's seventeen, and never backs off from a fight, especially with Perry, upon whom, I might add, she has on more than one occasion inflicted enough physical punishment to leave him crying uncle. "Is dear little Cheryl too good for the bus?"

"Dad!" Perry whines. "What kind of a guy takes a girl out on a date on a *bus*?" There's that cod-liver oil expression again. "I mean, I like to show a little class. I do have a reputation to uphold, you know."

Perry, I have to admit, has recently blossomed into a very good-looking guy, which has made him extremely popular with the girls at his high school, while also swelling his head to the size of a beach ball.

"Can you believe this guy?" Sia squawks. "A few girls give him a second look and all of a sudden he thinks he's a Greek god or something. Well, I don't care. There's a party at Dawn Kaplan's Saturday night and I don't want to be asking around for a ride when it's time to come home. Come on, Dad, you always say you don't want me taking rides with just anybody."

Mom and Dad have been following the proceedings like fans at a tennis match, their heads bobbing back and forth between Perry and Sia. They don't say anything, hoping, I guess, that Perry and Sia will be able to work this dispute out themselves.

Myself, I keep quiet, picking over my roast lamb and potatoes and mulling over just what I'm going to do with myself now that I'm captain of the boys' soccer team. But our kitchen's small, and as the three of us kids get older, it just seems to get even smaller. And more cramped. Staying out of one another's business isn't always easy.

"Mom!" Perry bellows.

"Dad!" Sia cries.

Believe me, with the noise level in our kitchen right now, it's hard to eat, let alone think.

Finally, Dad speaks up. I'm afraid he's going to start in with one of his lectures. Dad, you see, is a professor at the University of Manitoba in the Classics Department. He teaches Ancient Greek History and Literature, two subjects he seems never to have lectured enough about in class so he brings them up at home, too. If one of us has a problem we ask him about, he'll try to relate it to an Ancient Greek myth or something. In fact, Perry, Sia and I are all named after famous Ancient Greek figures. Perry is short for Pericles, a great statesman. Sia is short for Artemisia, who was supposed to be the goddess of hunting and also the protectress of young women. And my name, Lizzie, is short for Lysistrata, who was the title character in a play by someone named Aristophanes.

"I do see Perry's point," Dad says, "and yours, too, Sia. Perhaps we'll let Perry take the car, so he can impress this girl" — my dad winks at Perry just then — "and Sia, you can call me as soon as you're ready to come home and I'll come pick you up. We're not going anywhere Saturday night, Voula, are we?"

No lecture this time, I think. Whew!

"That's not fair!" Sia screeches.

"I have to agree with Sia, Paul," Mom offers. "They both have a good case, I suppose, but since Perry used the car last Saturday night ..."

"Mom!" Perry interrupts. "That was just to drive Uncle Ted to the airport!"

"Doesn't matter," Mom insists. "The point is, last Saturday night you used the car. This Saturday night, it's Sia's turn."

Sia's mouth breaks into a grin so wide it threatens to stretch right off her face.

"That doesn't settle anything," Perry continues. "Dad's on my side, and Mom's on Sia's side. That makes the vote two to two. It's even."

Uh-oh. I know what's coming next. My stomach does a backward double flip.

"Well," Dad begins in resignation, "I do like to think we make a lot of the important decisions in this family democratically, so I suppose we'll just have to turn to Lizzie for the deciding vote. Whatever she says, goes."

Here we go again, I think, as all eyes fix on me, anxiously awaiting my verdict.

You have to understand something about my family: for some reason or other, my dad and Perry are always teamed up against my mom and Sia, and I'm left to choose sides. Sometimes I think the only reason my parents had me was for situations like this, to break ties. You might think I just naturally take the girls' side, but that's not the case. Something inside me tells me I have to be as fair as possible, and I do my best to come up with the decision that makes the most sense. Luckily, nobody seems to resent me once I've made my decision, even if I've voted against them. They're just appreciative I'm around to help settle these little disputes. Mom and Dad tackle the big ones.

"Can't you guys handle this one without my help?" I ask Perry and Sia.

"No way," Perry pouts, "not if I want to be able to drive you to the mall Saturday afternoon."

"Don't listen to his bribes," Sia yelps. "We're sisters, Lizzie, and sisters stick together. This is an issue of women's rights."

"You've got to be kidding!" Perry jeers.

"I never kid around when it comes to sexual discrimination," Sia snaps, folding her arms tight around her chest and throwing him a nasty glare.

I suppose you could call Sia a feminist, especially since she calls herself one. I'm not sure yet if I'm one, but Sia does seem to have a point a lot of times, like last year when she managed to convince Dad and Perry that they couldn't just sit around at the dinner table after meals shooting the breeze while she, Mom and I cleared the table and loaded the dishwasher. Now, as a result, we all do the after-dinner chores together, they get done in half the time, and we have twice the fun doing them.

"Now, now," Mom breaks in, "let's not get carried away with this matter. I'm sure Lizzie understands what the issue is and she's perfectly capable of coming to a decision without your" — she stares down Perry and Sia — "interference."

"Thanks, Mom," I say. I take a gulp of milk and allow myself a few moments to consider Perry's and Sia's problem rather than my own. The way I see it, Perry can impress Cheryl by taking her out on a date in the car next weekend. But if Sia wants to make it home safely and before her eleven o'clock curfew, she could really use Mom's car.

"I've made up my mind," I say.

Sia and Perry slam down their cutlery and hold their breaths.

"Go ahead, honey," Dad says. "We're listening."

"Sia gets the car," I announce. "She needs it more."

"OK," Dad nods his head. "It's final. Sia, you can have the car Saturday night. Of course, you have to be home by eleven o'clock. As do you, Perry." Then he cracks a smile. "Only I suppose you might have to start back a little earlier as you'll be coming home on the bus."

"Ah, Dad, do you have to rub it in?"

"I'm only kidding."

Perry rolls his eyes.

Before long my family finishes up the meal and we all move to the sink with our dirty dishes. I figure this is as good a time as any to ask for some advice with my problem with the soccer team.

"Now that I've solved your problems," I say as Perry hands me a dish to place in the dishwasher, "maybe you guys can help me solve one of mine."

"What kind of problem could you have, kiddo?" Perry asks.

"It wouldn't be a boy problem, would it now, sis?" Sia chimes in.

"Actually," I say, "that's exactly what it is. A problem with a whole lot of boys."

I can see Mom and Dad's faces turn five shades of blue.

"Not *that* kind of boy problem," I say, trying to allay their fears.

"Well, what kind of boy problem, then, Lizzie?" Mom asks, still concerned.

"It's a long story."

"Give us the meaty parts," Perry says. "I just love to hear junior-high romance stories."

"This is *not* a romance story," I insist.

"Well, what is it exactly, Lizzie?" Dad asks.

I give it to them whole then, all the gruesome details, from Neena's cockamamie idea to play soccer to impress Justin all the way to the boys choosing me as the team captain. By the end of it all I'm just about in tears.

"So what I am I supposed to do?" I ask.

I draw a blank. Silence. The four of them look at one another like they can't believe quiet, smooth-sailing, tie-breaking, top-grade-making, sweet little Lizzie actually has a problem.

Finally, Sia pipes up.

"I say stick it to them. Be the best captain they ever had and don't settle for anything less. If they try kicking you off the team, take the matter to the school board, the local papers, all the way to the Supreme Court if you have to. This one is *definitely* an issue of women's rights."

I told you she could be feisty.

"I have to say I agree with Sia on this one, kiddo," Perry says. "Don't take any guff from those boys. They'll be sorry they ever made fun of a Lucas."

"Actually," I say, "the thought did occur to me that, no matter what Mr. Murray's decision is, I just might be best off quietly quitting the team along with the other girls and letting this incident slowly recede into the past."

Mom shakes her head.

"No way!" she blasts. Suddenly I realize where Sia gets her feistiness. "Don't let those boys bully you. If you want to play soccer with them, they can't stop you."

"Besides," Dad adds, "whether those boys realize it or not, you're the captain of the team. *You're* their leader. Go out there and show them what you're made of. I'll show you a trick or two with a soccer ball that'll leave those boys flat on their rear ends."

"Dad," I remind him, "*those boys* will be playing on my team."

"You know what I mean," Dad says. His face is red with anger. "I'm not telling you what to do, because this should be your decision, but if you do want to play soccer on that team, then do it."

Suddenly I understand what people mean when they say a family is "tightly knit." I know for sure now that's the way we are, and I feel good about it. It's like I'll be having my own personal cheering section if I decide to stay on with the boys' soccer team.

And I do believe I will. The boys wanted me to be their captain, and now they've got me as their captain. Like it or not.

6

Straight to the Principal's Office

First thing in the morning at school, before class, without telling Neena or any of the other girls, or even Coach Laughton or Coach Borowski, I march straight down to Mr. Murray's office. I'm there to take care of business.

"What can I do for you, dear?" the school secretary asks me. I don't think she recognizes me because the only time we've met was first term when my English teacher asked me to make thirty copies of my book report so our whole class could read it.

"I'd like to see Mr. Murray, please," I say. "School business."

"What kind of business?" the secretary asks. I decide she's nosy. "Is it a matter I can help you with?"

"I don't think so," I reply firmly. "It's kind of important."

The secretary shuffles a few papers on her desk and sneaks a look at the principal's day calendar.

"I'll go tell him you're coming." She heads toward his office, then makes a quick turn. "And your name was ...?"

"Lizzie Lucas," I answer. I knew she didn't remember me.

She pokes her head into Mr. Murray's office. After a few seconds, she turns to me. "OK. The principal will see you now."

Mr. Murray's office is neat and spacious, with an oak desk against one wall and a long couch and one armchair facing the desk. He has pictures of his kids on the desk: two girls and one boy, all teenagers. One of the girls is really pretty. On the wall, there's a painting of the Queen and a "Get High On Sports, Not Drugs" poster. I take a good look around because I've never been here before.

I've heard some ghastly stories about this place that made it sound like a Medieval torture chamber, but it looks pretty friendly to me. I suppose it all depends on your frame of mind when you walk through the doors.

For his part, Mr. Murray, who's tall and thin and reminds me of my pediatrician, eyes me up and down a few times, his fingers to his lips, thinking aloud, trying to recognize me. Of course, we've never met before this morning. Like I said, I've been keeping a really low profile.

"Lizzie Lucas," he mumbles to himself, squinting at me through his wire-rimmed glasses. "Lizzie Lucas... Lucas, Lizzie... Lucas ..." He shakes his head.

"I'm in grade seven," I say, helping him out. "Ms. Bernstein is my home-room and History teacher."

He slaps his forehead lightly with the palm of his right hand.

"Of course. Lizzie Lucas." This time when he says the name, it seems to ring a bell somewhere inside his head. "Straight A's, I've been told, and an absolute pleasure to teach."

"That's me," I say shyly. "But I did get a C+ in Music first term."

Mr. Murray chuckles and shakes my hand.

"Sometimes I think you have to be a troublemaker to get noticed around here," he says thoughtfully. "It's a shame, it really is."

I just nod my head.

"Have a seat, Lizzie." He extends his hand towards the couch, then seats himself behind his desk. "And what exactly is the nature of your visit?"

"Well, I'm actually here as captain of the school soccer team," I say. The cushions on the couch sink real low and I have to look up to speak to him.

"Is that so? Good for you, Lizzie. And how does our girls' soccer team look this year? Do we have a chance to make the finals?"

I bring my hand up to my mouth to cover a nervous cough.

"As a matter of fact, Mr. Murray," I state, "there is no girls' soccer team this year. There weren't enough girls out for the first practice. I'm the captain of the *boys'* soccer team."

I let that information sink in for a few beats. Mr. Murray sits behind his desk in what you might call stunned silence.

"Anyhow," I continue, "that's why I'm here. You see, we girls — there are five of us — we really want to play on this team. At least try out for it, just like the other boys. But Coach Borowski said he has to get your permission first. He thinks there are probably regulations forbidding girls from playing on the boys' teams. I'm here to make sure we get your permission. We really want this chance."

Believe me, I'm really surprising myself — the way I'm talking, I mean. So easily, so freely, like I sit down and chat with the school principal every other morning.

"I believe there might be some outdated regulations to that effect," Mr. Murray begins. "You know, nothing like this has ever been done before, to my knowledge, here at Corydon Junior High School."

"I can understand that," I say. I'm really on a roll right now. "But it just doesn't seem fair that we can't play with the boys if we want to. And we do. The opportunity to try out for the boys' soccer team means a lot to us girls. We don't want to back off now."

Mr. Murray leans back on his leather swivel chair and closes his eyes, the fingers of his two hands tented in front of his lips.

"If you girls are really serious about this — and by the sounds of it, you are," he says, "I'm sure there won't be any real problem allowing you to play on the boys' soccer team."

I lean forward, excited.

"What I'm trying to say is," Mr. Murray continues, "I'll back you up." I can tell he's on our side. It shows in the fire that suddenly lights up his eyes. "Frankly, Lizzie, I'm impressed with the sense of conviction you've expressed to me here today. As well, you have a great reputation among the teachers in this school, whether you've been noticed by me or not" — he chuckles again — "and on account of that I think I owe it to you to do everything in my power to make this happen for you and the other girls. When's your next practice?"

"Friday after school." My heart's a steam engine.

"I'll have the official permission slips prepared by then." He shakes my hand again, which is something, I'm beginning to realize, boys and men do a lot of. It feels good.

"Thanks," I say. "I really appreciate your efforts."

"I'm sure you'll make a great team captain, Lizzie Lucas."

I blush. Mr. Murray smiles at me.

I can hardly contain my joy. I perform a quick spin off the couch, like a ballerina's curtain-falling pirouette, and make my way out of Mr. Murray's office. I'm walking on air. I can't wait to tell Neena and the other girls the good news.

"Goodbye, Lizzie," the secretary addresses me warmly as I stride out of the office. "Have a good day."

I just smile back at her. I'm starting to think that maybe it is worth speaking out every once in a while. It's really the only way to get heard.

7

Boys Will Be Boys

Over lunch that same day I tell Neena the good news about Mr. Murray's promise to do his best for the girls. We're at a deli that makes huge, juicy falafels we like to share whenever we have some extra money.

"There's nothing stopping us now," Neena says. Tahini sauce is squiggling out the corners of her mouth, and she stretches out her tongue to lick it back in. "That soccer team is our ticket to success."

"Well," I remind her, "there is the small matter of the boys. I don't know about you, but I received the distinct impression that they weren't too eager to share their team with us." I chomp into my half of the falafel.

"That's true," Neena admits, "but they'll come around."

"What makes you so sure?" I ask.

"Because they're not all that bad." Neena's sapphire eyes sparkle. "Remember, Justin did help me up when I took that awful spill."

Of course she'd remember that incident. I begin to hope Neena's mind isn't so much on Justin that she forgets we still have to actually earn our spots on the boys' soccer team.

"Maybe they will come around," I say. "Enzo was pretty nice to me during the heading drill. Still, I'm a little worried about Friday afternoon's practice."

"We're practising with your dad after school today, right?" Neena offers. "I'm sure that'll help prepare us."

"It will. But we need a whole lot of work."

"I'm willing. I'm finding soccer a lot of fun. I can see why it's your favourite sport."

"I'm glad," I say. And I mean it. I enjoy introducing Neena to new things just as she's introduced me to a lot of new things. It's also a relief to hear her make a real commitment to soccer.

"This is going to work out even better than we planned," Neena goes on, taking a last bite of falafel and wiping her fingers with a paper napkin. "Soon the whole school will want to be our friends."

At precisely that moment, Jasmine strolls into the deli along with Kayla, the class beauty queen. As they scan the place for a spot to sit down, Neena and I look up at them and smile. Jasmine's eyes meet mine, and she and Kayla start walking towards us. I open my mouth to ask them to sit down with us. But before I get the words out, Kayla struts by us without even saying a word, and Jasmine follows obediently right behind. She doesn't even look back. The two of them take a seat with two skateboarder boys from grade eight.

"I see what you mean," I remark sarcastically to Neena. I take a final gurgling slurp through the straw of my iced tea. "Already kids are jumping across tables and booths just to meet us."

"Give it some time," Neena insists. "Everything will work out."

As we leave the deli, I don't say anything. What is there to say? We just have to give this soccer business some time and see what comes of it. What I do know, though, is that I could never go through anything like this without Neena at my side. I guess that's what being friends is all about, helping each other be as fully yourself as possible.

That afternoon, as planned, we practise with my dad. I know he's keen about teaching us his soccer tricks when he steps out into the backyard wearing his old Ilisiakos jersey and shorts and a worn-out pair of cleats. He always complains about Perry not appreciating soccer, so I guess I'm Dad's last hope to carry on the family soccer tradition.

After a few moments, we get down to business. Dad says that our primary concern should be ball control.

"Control the ball, and you control the game," Dad points out.

We stand at one end of the yard and he kicks the ball to us from all sorts of angles. Some passes arrive on the ground, some after one or two bounces, some high in the air, some low. His accuracy is amazing. Our job is to trap the ball and pass it back to him quickly.

That's not as easy as it might sound. One of his kicks knocks me in the shoulder and I fall to the ground as the ball bounces over the next-door neighbour's fence. Another glances off Neena's ankle and ricochets against our kitchen window. There's no broken glass, but my mom does warn Dad to keep the ball a little lower.

Before long, Neena and I are managing quite well. The key is to decide almost automatically what part of your body you'll use to trap the ball and then make sure you adjust yourself so that the ball kind of sinks into your body and then falls straight in front of you.

Dad points out what we're doing wrong and what we're doing right. He's especially impressed when I use my head to butt one of his kicks right back to him and when Neena finally masters the foot trap, which is probably the best way to stop a rolling ball, just by stepping on it. It's a very basic soccer skill, but Neena has to start some place. The point is, she's trying. At least she won't be tripping over the ball next time we have to practise with the boys.

By the end of our session, all three of us have established a neat rhythm, Dad kicking the ball to us and Neena and I returning it to him in easy, fluid motions. If we were in a game right now, I think, we'd be scoring a whole lot of goals. The boys had better look out Friday afternoon.

After we change back into our street clothes, Dad drives us to the video store to rent a movie to watch at Neena's house. We choose *Love Story*, which we've both seen about five times but never tire of. Neena's mom makes us some lentil soup to eat (something else our families have in common, though Neena's mom's recipe is spicier than my mom's), and then the three of us sit down and cry our eyes out. It's that kind of movie, about a rich guy who falls in love with a poor girl who's dying of cancer. For ninety minutes at least, our minds are off soccer, which is just what we need. There's such a thing as getting over-psyched.

And then, before we know it, it's Friday afternoon — time for our first official practice with the boys.

Neena and I arrive at the practice field together. The boys are bunched at the far goal net, and Melanie is off by herself at the nearest goal net, just juggling a soccer ball with her feet and body, tuned out to the rest of the world. Neither of the other girls has shown up yet. I begin to worry that maybe they've decided to quit.

My dad always says that May is the best month to be in Winnipeg, and today supports that claim. It's hot, but not too hot. The sun is out, and a gentle, cooling breeze is stirring the leaves on the stand of trees separating the soccer field from the baseball diamond. Even better, there are no mosquitoes zinging about yet.

In fact, for a moment I think maybe Neena and I are crazy to be out on this field right now, ready to play soccer with a bunch of boys who don't even want us on their team. We could be riding our bikes over the monkey trails alongside the river in Assiniboine Park, or enjoying a cone of gelati at the Italian grocery, or even picking another movie to watch at the video store.

But that wouldn't be nearly as much fun as this, I decide finally. We're breaking new ground today.

Eventually Jasmine and Natalie show up. I sigh with relief. Natalie is wearing knee pads and leather gloves. She says she wants to try out for the goaltending position. Jasmine is digging into the dirt with the toes of her brand-new cleats, breaking them in. I realize I never did have to worry about these girls' sense of determination. They're as gung-ho as I could ever have hoped.

"Why don't you guys take a few shots on me until Coach Borowski shows up?" Natalie asks.

We form a circle and take turns booting the ball at her. I suspect that even Jasmine has been practising on her own a bit, because she delivers some nice volleys at Natalie. Neena hits the goalpost on a low drive that sends Natalie diving through the dirt. I'm proud of her. And Melanie scores a goal on a powerful shot that flies right through Natalie's hands.

"I think you guys are getting pretty good at this!" Natalie enthuses.

The boys, meanwhile, are doing their own thing, trying to ignore us, as if we don't exist. They're pounding the ball hard at Victor, who's playing goalie, trying to prove — I think — how much stronger they are than us. But, from what I can see, a lot of their shots are way off the mark, zooming high over the crossbar or metres to either side of the posts.

"OK, everyone," Coach Borowski announces as he jogs onto the field, "gather round so we can get this practice under way."

The boys rush in, and so do we.

"Ah, Coach," Victor snarls, "I thought you said the girls wouldn't be here this practice."

"I didn't say that, Victor," Coach snaps back. "I said I'd see whether or not having the girls on the team was against the regulations of the school board."

"Well?" Brad asks, as if the answer should be obvious.

"Well, I don't know yet. Mr. Murray is looking into the matter and promised me he'll know for sure sometime today."

Neena and I share a secret glance. We're pretty sure Mr. Murray will pull through for us.

Coach Borowski smiles at the girls then, as if he's pleasantly surprised that we've shown up for today's practice. I guess he thought that maybe the boys' behaviour last practice would have been enough to discourage us. Now he'll know we're made of tougher stuff than that.

"Anyway," he continues, "it's time to get down to some soccer, which is why we're all here in the first place. I think we'll start with two-on-one drills and then maybe end the practice with a scrimmage."

I have to admit Coach Borowski, now that he's fully involved, is an excellent soccer coach. As he explains the two-on-one drill, I get the idea he knows exactly what he's talking about. When he takes a few demonstration shots, I'm reminded of my father's kicking form.

At each end of the field he sets up one goalie (Victor on one end and Natalie on the other) and then two players try to move in on a defender, passing between them and taking a shot on net. When they've taken a shot, another two attackers get the ball and the chance to move in on net against the next defender. The attacker who actually takes the final shot on net or loses the ball to the defender, gets in line to be a defender next time around.

My first time up I'm on the attack with Neena against Brad, with Natalie in net. Coach starts the drill off by tossing the ball at Neena's feet. I guess she's a little nervous still, because she acts like the last thing she wants just then is a soccer ball at her feet. She toes the ball hurriedly back to me and moves downfield, glad, I can tell, that the pressure is momentarily off her.

I trap the ball with the sole of my foot and start dribbling forward, tapping the ball lightly from one foot to the next, all the time cutting towards the net, keeping my eyes on Neena's positioning.

I look directly forward then and see that Brad has his eyes set on me like a dog who's just been commanded to "Sic 'er!" He charges towards me, his legs pumping like pistons.

I try to keep my cool. I know that if I get nervous and start looking down at my feet and not in front of me at Brad, he'll steal the ball away. And I'm not about to try anything fancy like a shoulder-fake because I'm liable to make an absolute fool of myself. So I just keep dribbling forward, head up, feet and knees protecting the ball.

Control the ball, I keep repeating to myself, and you control the game.

Suddenly, Brad lunges at me.

I tap the ball forward, trying to direct it between his outstretched legs.

I do. The ball sneaks past him like a croquet ball through a wire loop.

He tries to turn back. But his right leg's still lunged forward. With his two legs trying to move in opposite directions, he loses his balance and plunks to the ground.

All I have to do now is run around him to the ball. I bend my knees and begin my move. I keep my eyes up and see Neena breaking for the net. Good for her, I think. As soon as I regain control of the ball, I'll send it over to her.

And then, out of nowhere, Brad, who's still on the ground, manages to prop up one of his feet between mine. It's so fast I hardly realize what has happened to me. To Coach Borowski and the others on the team, it probably looks like I just got tripped up over my own two feet in my hurry to reach the ball. But I can feel Brad's cleat dig hard into my shin.

I go flying forward in a swan dive. Just imagine a wooden stick being jammed in between the spokes of a moving bicycle and you'll have some idea of what happens to me. My face lands first, my mouth getting an unwanted taste of freshly mown green grass. Then my knees take a metre-long scrape against the ground. I feel the pain immediately. It takes all the strength I have to hold back a scream.

Meanwhile, Brad pushes himself up and races Neena for the ball. She hooks back to the ball, but too slowly to beat Brad. He reaches the ball first and steps down hard on it, like a conquering warrior staking a claim on enemy land. Then he boots the ball far out of bounds. All the guys who've seen the drill howl with delight. Brad has succeeded in stopping our two-on-one and making the girls appear ineffective.

I rub my shin with the palm of my hand, trying to ease the pain. There's a purple bruise taking form there like an instant photo developing right before my eyes. I try to take a deep breath, but almost gag. Sure enough, I swoosh my tongue around inside my mouth and come up with a tuft of grass. I spit that out disgustedly.

Neena races to my side.

"Are you all right?"

"I guess so," I lie. "Except I've lost all feeling in my right shin and I've just had the pleasure of snacking on raw grass."

"That was a good move you used to thread the ball between Brad's leg."

"How about Brad's move to thread his leg between my feet?"

"No way!"

I guess Neena didn't catch Brad's sneaky leg work either.

"I'm afraid so. These boys aren't above playing dirty. We'd better be prepared."

By then Jasmine has joined Neena at my side and helps me up.

"Shake it off, Lizzie. You'll be OK."

Out on the soccer field, I guess, Jasmine's not so concerned with who's popular and who's not. One good thing about playing with the boys is that now all us girls seem a lot closer.

I get up and trot over to the defender's line. As I take my place behind Enzo, the next pair of players begins a two-on-one.

"That was a nasty trip," he says.

"Yeah, right," I say. "Like you care. You guys are out to kill us today."

"What are you talking about?" Enzo protests.

For a second I consider the possibility once again that maybe all the boys aren't in on this.

But I dismiss that possibility when during the next two-on-one Tyler McNaught, who's been paired with Jasmine, hogs the ball all the way to the net, as if she's not even there to pass to, and then takes a boot at the net that misses the crossbar by about five metres. Cooperation is obviously not in the vocabulary of these particular players.

But cooperation is something they're going to have to learn because just as I'm getting ready to defend against Neena and Justin, who just *happen* to be paired together, Mr. Murray jogs out onto the field in his three-piece suit, waving a long piece of paper above his head. When he sees me, he smiles.

"Hi, Lizzie! How's it going?" He winks at me and immediately I know he's bearing good news.

"Fine, Mr. Murray." I talk to him like we're old pals. I can tell the rest of the girls, and even some of the boys, are impressed.

He walks straight to Coach Borowski and shows him the piece of paper. Everybody stops what they're doing and edges closer to Mr. Murray and Coach Borowski, trying to see what the piece of paper says.

It's a real official-looking paper — you could safely call it a document — with two big blue rubber stamps on it. But none of us can read exactly what it says.

Coach Borowski nods his head slowly and then shakes Mr. Murray's hand. Mr. Murray jogs back off the field. Coach Borowski holds up the piece of paper.

"Here in my hand, ladies and gentlemen," he says, "I hold the official permission for these five girls to try out for the Corydon Junior High School boys' soccer team."

A few boys send up a loud groan.

Jasmine shouts "All right!"

"I don't want to hear anything more about this matter," Coach commands. "There'll be no whining, *and* there'll be no gloating. The decision is final. Let us — please! — get back to playing soccer."

Jasmine can't help herself. She jumps up and down and pats me on the back. She's not exactly gloating, just celebrating.

Coach Borowski resumes the practice by calling a scrimmage game. Melanie, Neena and I are on one team, Jasmine and Natalie on the other. Wise move, I think, mixing the boys with the girls. That way we'll be forced to learn to cooperate.

But am I ever wrong! Because if I thought the boys had been playing dirty up to then, I was misguided. During the scrimmage game that follows, I come to understand just how dirty dirty can get.

No matter what the official teams are, the real game that's going on is still the boys against the girls. Let me give you a brief run-through of the boys' fiendish tactics.

At one point, as Melanie is attacking, Brad has to back-track to keep up with her and appears to be losing the battle. She swings around him to his right and makes a break for the net. At the last second, however, Brad hip-checks Melanie off the ball, sending her butt-first into the grass.

Coach Borowski was explaining something to Jasmine just then, so he doesn't see a thing. Brad collects the ball and heads for the centre line. Of course, that doesn't stop Melanie from getting right back up, chasing down Brad, tackling the ball away from him the way the pros do it on TV — by sliding into him and propping the ball loose from his feet — and barrelling straight for the net, scoring a goal on a volley shot right over Natalie's head.

That makes it one to nothing for our team.

And this time Coach Borowski does see the goal, all the way from Melanie's steal from Brad to the ball cutting the plane of the goal line.

"Way to go, Melanie," Coach shouts. "That's the kind of ball-playing I'm looking for today."

Next, Tyler, who's on my team, gives me a shove so that I fall right on top of Jasmine as she's trying to defend against me. We scramble over each other on the ground, and Tyler snags the ball away from me, moving down the field with a big grin on his face like he's just accomplished something great.

"This stinks!" I hear Melanie mutter to herself.

Later, when I go up for a header off one of Justin's corner kicks, I feel Tyler's elbow stab into my spine and wilt to the ground as the ball passes overhead. These boys are relentless.

But Neena is on the receiving end of possibly the worst example of the boys' unsportsmanlike behaviour.

On a two-on-one breakaway with Justin, she tries to deke around Brad so she can make a clean pass to Justin. Brad knees her hard right in the stomach. I cringe as I witness the infraction. Neena doubles over and falls to the ground, gasping for breath. Brad has hit her so hard she's winded. Coach Borowski runs to her and helps her up, telling her to draw some slow, deep breaths.

"You can quit for the day, Neena," he says. "I'm sorry this had to happen."

"I'll be OK, Coach," Neena manages to pant when her wind is back. "I want to keep on playing."

Coach Borowski nods his head. "OK, girl. You sure do have a lot of guts."

All of us girls are gathered around Neena and he looks at us all, nodding his head the same way.

"You've all got guts," he says, loud enough so that everybody on the field can hear him. He's not just talking to us, but to the boys, too. "As far as I'm concerned each and every one of you girls can be assured of making this team. You're tough and you know how to fight adversity. Those are the kind of players we need around here."

Victor hisses. Tyler kicks at the turf. I feel a flying pebble sting the back of my leg.

"That's enough for today," Coach goes on. "We're not accomplishing much, anyway."

Brad cuts in then.

"Coach, can we at least have another vote for captain? We were just fooling the other day when we picked her." He points at me with a scowl on his face. "I nominate Justin."

"I second that nomination," Tyler calls out.

Justin stands there stunned. I get the feeling he wants to tell the boys he'd rather not be captain, but he can't quite muster up the courage.

Coach Borowski speaks up again, shaking his head.

"Absolutely not," he says. "Lizzie Lucas is still our captain. The final roster will be posted outside my office Monday morning. Everybody who finds their name there is to meet after school in front of the school to take the bus to Crescentwood Junior High for our first game. I hope by then the boys who are left on this team will have learned the value of cooperation."

Melanie, Natalie, Jasmine, Neena and I are all banged up — bruised thighs, skinned knees, sore backs and stubbed toes.

But we're happy. We're the only ones out on the field who know for sure that we've made the team.

8

Aches and Pains

Saturday mornings at my house are usually a whole lot of fun. Basically, all the rules are changed: there are none. For example, every other day, Sia wakes up before seven o'clock, takes a shower, and readies herself for school. But on Saturdays she sleeps in until about noon, and then loafs around the house in her pyjamas. It's the one day of the week I get to see her hair messed up and stringy.

And Perry is allowed to play his stereo as loud as he likes. Which he does. You can almost see the sound waves from the rap music he listens to pounding against the walls of the house. Beats me how Sia can sleep through that noise, but she does.

Competing with Perry's rap music is Mom's Greek music, coming from the radio-cassette player Perry, Sia and I bought her last year for Christmas, which she keeps in the basement to listen to while she does laundry or irons clothes. The music is jangly and electric, made mostly by an instrument called a *bouzouki*, which looks kind of like a guitar only it's a lot rounder. Sometimes I like Mom's music, and sometimes I can't stand it. Depends what mood I'm in.

Dad's always the first one to wake up, and he cooks breakfast for everybody, letting it sit in the oven to keep warm. He usually makes his famous French toast from a recipe he learned while he worked in the Winnipeg Hotel restaurant (it's chewy and cinnamony, and I like to smother it in maple syrup). As each of us wakes up, we know to just look in the oven and help ourselves to Dad's homemade breakfast.

In the meantime, he sits at the kitchen table and pores over the Saturday newspaper, line by line. I think he even reads each and every classified listing, whether he's in the market for what's being advertised or not. It's just a thing with him, I guess, to know that Saturday paper inside and out. He'll spend the rest of the day, whether he's doing yard work or helping Mom clean the house, starting conversations with all of us that begin with the words: "You know what I read today in the paper?"

Me, I usually like to wake up at about ten o'clock. I'll watch some cartoons on TV, even the real kids' stuff, because it reminds me of when I was just a kid. Not that I'm a senior citizen now, but I think you know what I mean. Watching kids' shows makes you feel like everything in the world's all right and that's a nice feeling to have every once in a while.

Sometimes I'll grab the comics section from Dad's paper and spend time chuckling to myself over the especially funny comics. There's something special about laughing all by yourself.

This morning, though, when I push myself out of bed, I'm not in the mood for cartoons or comics. In fact, I'm not in the mood for anything. My body is so sore from soccer practice the day before that I can hardly move. My shoulders are numb, and my legs feel like they've been pulverized. It takes all my strength just to stand up and make my way to the bathroom. Those boys sure did a number on us, bumping us around like cars at a smash-up derby.

I smell Dad's French toast in the air and head for the kitchen. But when I bend down to the oven to pull out the toast, I have the hardest time straightening back up. I must look like an elderly person who's lost his cane. As I grunt with pain, Dad takes notice of me, lifting his eyes from last night's NHL playoff scores.

"Lizzie, what's happened to you?" he asks, obviously concerned.

"Soccer practice happened to me," I reply curtly.

I don't have the energy to explain just then. I collapse into a chair at the kitchen table, setting my plate down carefully. When I stretch out to reach for the syrup, my right side burns up like someone lit a flame underneath it.

"Aaaagggh!" That's called a shriek of pain. My whole body feels like one big throbbing ache.

"I remember I'd feel pretty beat up after my practices," Dad offers, "but this is ridiculous. You're only twelve years old. How hard can a practice be at that age?"

"Hard, Dad, very hard. Especially when you're playing against boys."

"They took cheap shots at you, didn't they?" I can see Dad is getting worked up.

By way of an answer, I lift my pyjama leg up over my right knee. The evidence is all right there. A bruise the colour of a plum on the side of my shin. And Victor's cleat marks like a tattoo over my ankle.

Dad springs immediately beside me and rubs my shin and ankle. I wince in pain.

"You'll be OK," Dad assures me, like he knows what he's talking about. "At least your foot's not swollen."

That makes me feel a little better.

"I think you should soak those feet in some warm water, though." Dad rises to the sink and runs the taps, his hand below the faucet testing the water temperature. "That's what I used to do to get rid of the soreness after a game."

Dad brings a tub of warm water to me and I plunge my feet inside. Right away I feel the pain oozing out like a slow leak from a bicycle tire.

"That's much better," I sigh.

"Good." Dad wipes his hands on a dishcloth. "I'm sure you'll be fine by next practice. I guess those boys have never heard of the Amazons."

We share a laugh. The Amazons were a group of legendary warrior women who defeated any men who tried to invade their island. Being compared to them after battling with the boys in practice is just fine with me.

I'm glad Dad just seems to know now even without asking that I'm not about to quit the soccer team. As rough as the boys played, to tell the truth, I still enjoyed myself. Soccer is fun, plain and simple. There's always some sort of action on the field, which I like because it makes for a lot of excitement. In football, there's all those stops and starts. In baseball, you have to wait your turn to get up to the plate and swing the bat. Not so in soccer. At any time you can run down the ball and make a play to score a goal.

What's more, soccer is wonderfully simple. There's just a bunch of players, a ball, and two nets. Why complicate things with sticks and bats and helmets? I mean, I never have liked ringette because those pointy sticks and the rubber ring always seemed goofy to me. Same goes for field hockey sticks, with their curved blades that don't really let you control the ball. Soccer's just soccer. I appreciate that.

The best thing about soccer is the feel of the ball against your feet, the sense that you have some sort of control over it without using your hands. Sometimes when you're dribbling down the field, you don't even have to look down at your feet to make sure the ball is there. Your feet do all your thinking for you. That's neat.

Frankly, I know that with a little more practice the rest of the girls and I could fit right into the boys' team. We're all decent players, and we're dedicated to improving. We're willing to work hard and do whatever it takes to become better soccer players. All we need is a fair chance.

As I sop my last scrap of French toast in a puddle of syrup, I wonder if we'll get that chance in our opening game Thursday night.

With my feet soaking in the warm water, I decide to ask my father if he'll let me buy some soccer cleats. I know they're expensive, but I think I'll be able to play a lot better with them. I won't go sliding all over the field when I try to make sharp turns and I think I'll be able to hit the ball a little harder.

"Dad, I have a favour to ask you," I say. He's in the middle of trying for the one-hundredth time to make sense of the baseball box scores in the newspaper. He never gives up on anything. "I think I'd like to buy some soccer cleats."

By now Mom is upstairs and she's pulling the vacuum cleaner out of the kitchen closet where we keep all the cleaning supplies. She's a lot tighter with the purse strings than Dad, so I kind of wish she'd just get on with her housework. But no such luck.

"Soccer cleats!" she exclaims. "I saw some advertised in the flyer last week. They cost as much as seventy dollars!"

"Thanks, Mom," I mumble.

Mom, you see, is a real wise shopper. Too wise, for my liking. When I grocery shop with Dad, he'll buy anything I ask for no matter how expensive or far-out. For example, a few weeks ago we bought this weird-looking fruit called a papaya. I didn't end up liking it, but it was worth trying. Mom never would have bought it. She always has a ready answer whenever I make an unusual request at the grocery store. "You won't like that, I know," she'll say, or "That's not necessary," or "It's not a good value for the money." If it's up to her, I just know I won't get those cleats.

"Well, if Lizzie needs new cleats," Dad reasons, "perhaps we should buy them for her. She *is* putting a lot of effort into playing soccer. I'm proud of her."

"So am I," Mom answers. "But are cleats really necessary?"

There she goes again, I think.

"I think so," Dad continues. "They might help prevent further injury." Dad nods towards me and my soaking feet.

"Oh, my gosh!" Mom squeals when she notices my feet swimming in the tub of warm water. "Are you all right?"

"Nothing a new pair of soccer cleats couldn't cure," I remark.

Mom laughs. I can tell she's softening on the soccer cleats.

"The boys banged us up a little last practice," I continue. "But I can take it. If I had some soccer cleats, though, I think I'd do a lot better."

"It's not like a pair of cleats is going to turn you into an instant soccer star." Mom's not only a wise shopper, she's also, unfortunately, very logical.

"Of course not," Dad says. "But they will give her added traction on the field. And if they make her feel better, she'll probably play better." He rises to empty out the kitchen garbage.

"OK, OK," Mom relents. She moves to the cupboard over the stove and pulls a bunch of paper bills out of this little replica of an Ancient Greek vase where she keeps the family's spending cash. "Here's seventy-five dollars, Lizzie. You can go to the mall today and pick out a pair. Perry can drive you. He's running a few errands for me with the car this afternoon."

"Sorry, but no go." That's Perry. He's just walked into the room wearing his baby-blue terry-cloth bathrobe. Red shaving nicks spot his face. His hair is freshly shampooed.

"I'm in too much of a hurry," he explains. "I want to be back early to get ready for my date."

"How long's that going to take?" Mom asks, making a face. "You've already shaved and showered."

She can't believe how long Perry takes to get ready to go out. He's usually in the bathroom combing his hair and fixing his clothes twice as long as anybody else in the family. Sometimes I think the mirror is his best friend.

"It'll take long, believe me. I'm not even sure what I'm going to wear yet. Can't Lizzie take the bus? *I* have to tonight."

Perry eyes me coldly. I get the idea it's payback time for me for voting to let Sia use the car tonight rather than him. Maybe I should have taken him up on his bribe.

Just then the phone rings. Mom twists to answer it, her feet tangled in the vacuum cleaner cord, her left hand holding a cardboard box of carpet cleaner.

"Hello?" Mom sets the carpet cleaner down and steps out of the looped cord. "Yes, Lizzie is home. Can I ask who's calling?"

I don't know about you, but I hate it when my Mom asks that. Who does she think it's going to be? The prime minister?

"Lizzie," Mom calls, "it's Natalie."

Natalie? Why would she be calling? I lug my bruised body over to the phone and snatch it from Mom's hand.

"Hi," I squeak into the phone.

"Hi, Lizzie." Natalie sounds as if she calls me every Saturday morning. "How you doing?"

"Tired and beat up from yesterday's practice."

"Oh, right, that was tough wasn't it? But we did all right."

"I hope we do even better on Thursday."

"So do I."

There's a pause. I look around and notice that even though they're acting like they're doing housework, my family's listening in on my conversation. They're all snoops, every one of them. Then again, so am I a lot of the time. I decide to let it pass.

"Listen, Lizzie," Natalie goes on, "I'm taking the bus to Portage Place this afternoon, and I was wondering whether you'd like to come along."

I can't believe it! One of the most popular girls in school and she's asking me, Lizzie Lucas, to go to the mall with her. Maybe this soccer thing will work out just as Neena said it would, after all.

"Sure," I say. "I have to go downtown anyway to buy a new pair of cleats." I try not to sound too enthusiastic. "Just let me ask my dad if it's OK if I take the bus."

I press my hand tightly over the phone speaker and look pleadingly at Dad.

"Dad, please, pretty please, pretty please with a cherry on top, will you let me take the bus to Portage Place with Natalie — she's a friend from school on the soccer team with me?"

My parents rarely let me go to the mall without one of them or Sia or Perry. But this time I have a feeling Dad, at the very least, might give in. He feels sorry for me, I guess, and I know he's excited about my playing soccer. I'm already thinking I can't wait to drop by and pick up Neena at her dad's jewelry store. This is just the kind of opportunity we've been looking forward to.

"You'll be careful?" Dad asks. "And back by two o'clock?"

It's looking good! I try my best not to scream for joy.

"Of course," I say, as composed as possible.

"And you'll call from Mr. Raman's store as soon as you arrive at the mall and when you're ready to leave?" Mom adds.

"Yes, yes," I answer. Give me a break, I think. I mean, in less than a year I'll be a teenager, and my parents are still worrying about me taking the bus downtown.

"Then it's fine with me, if it's fine with your mom," Dad states.

I turn to Mom, my face screwed up into one big "PLEASE!"

"OK," she mutters.

"All right!" I shout.

My parents eye me like they're both thinking, "Is this the same daughter who was living in this house last week?"

I unclasp my hand from the phone and tell Natalie the good news.

"It's OK with my folks," I say. "Where do we meet?"

Natalie gives me the details and then hangs up. I jump for joy. My feet, however, land inside the tub of warm water. Water goes splashing up into Mom's face.

"You're feeling better already," Mom observes, smiling.

"I think so," I admit.

I leap out of the tub and race for my room. The pain from the soccer practice is still there, I'm just not noticing it as much as before.

What am I going to wear? What will we talk about? I wonder if any of the other kids will see us together? Does this mean I'm part of the popular crowd?

I'm asking myself so many crazy questions I can hardly get dressed. I keep jamming the buttons of my blouse into the wrong holes and my over-excited fingers almost yank the zipper right off my blue denim overalls.

But it doesn't matter. Because I can smell popularity right around the corner. In fact, to commemorate the occasion, I decide to leave the right strap on my overalls unsnapped, just kind of flapping against my body, the way the cool girls at school do.

Why not? All of a sudden, I feel cool, too.

9

One of the Girls

It feels neat sitting on the bus next to Natalie. Different. Like I'm somebody special. Maybe it's my imagination, but I get the sense suddenly that I'm being noticed.

Sure enough, in the next moment I catch two boys who are sitting a few seats ahead of us glancing back every so often like they're trying to work up the courage to come talk to us. If this is what it's like being part of the cool crowd, I think, then I like it!

Natalie looks fabulous. She's wearing a brocaded brown and gold floral print mini-dress stretched over black tights. Gold and silver bracelets are looped around her wrists, and a black pillbox hat is perched impishly on her head.

"I hope I get a chance to play in net our first game," Natalie says. Of course, I'm having a tough time right now picturing Natalie, primped as she is, as a soccer goaltender. But I like that about her. Not always being stuck playing one role, I mean. Just like I'm a lot more than just a good student. But, unfortunately, I never get a chance to show it.

"I hope we all get to start," I say. "And I think we deserve it. We've really worked hard."

"I've enjoyed it," Natalie continues. She has bright blue eyes and a warm smile. "Trying out for the boys' team has really been fun. I'm glad you thought of it."

I can't believe it! Not only am I sitting on the bus with Natalie Lundstrom but she's also throwing compliments my way. Life's really looking up for me, no question about it. Maybe my grade seven year can still be saved.

Just then the bus wheezes to a stop. The doors fold open and in walk Jasmine and Kayla.

"Hey, girls, over here!" Natalie calls out from her seat.

Jasmine and Kayla notice Natalie and head our way. They teeter a little as the bus pushes back onto the road. They spill into the seat ahead of ours and turn back to see us. Jasmine greets Natalie and me.

"What's going on?" Kayla enquires. She's wearing dark eye shadow and reddish black lipstick.

"What do you mean?" Natalie asks.

"Since when did you guys start hanging out with *her*?" Kayla sniffs, nodding her chin in my direction.

"Since soccer," Natalie says. "As a matter of fact, it was Lizzie here who came up with the idea for us girls to try out for the boys' team." Jasmine doesn't say anything. I think she's waiting to see Kayla's reaction before she commits her support my way. Like I said before, she subscribes to the follow-the-leader philosophy of winning popularity.

"Whatever suits you, I guess," Kayla mutters. "Personally, I think there are better things to do with boys than play soccer."

"You'd be surprised," I crack. "Don't be fooled thinking that soccer isn't a contact sport." That smart little remark earns me a chuckle from Natalie and Kayla. Once again I've surprised myself by opening my mouth.

The laughter seems to break the ice. Before long, I think Kayla forgets she's sitting with Lizzie Lucas, class bookworm. The conversation among the four of us flows easily, from boys to fashion to school to you-name-it. Even though

I'm not doing too much of the talking, I'm having a lot of fun just listening.

These girls seem to know where all the action is at Corydon Junior High School. They discuss upcoming house parties that I've never even heard mention of. They gossip about the teachers' private lives. And they seem to know everything there is to know about the love life in our school. Which boy is going out with which girl and what they've done together. Who's asking whom to the next dance.

It's like there's this whole other level of existence to the boys and girls of my class that up to now I haven't had the foggiest clue about. Like Natasha Plotkin smooching with Frank Miller on the way home from school last week. Or Alexis Donato having the nerve to spell out I LUV U in red lipstick on the outside of Justin's bedroom window. Wait until I tell Neena, I think. She'll love this stuff. It's refreshing to get a winner's-eye-view of school life for a change.

At Portage Place, we head straight for Generation X, which is this super-cool clothing store. I want to find Neena so she can join us and I also need to call my parents, but I can't pull myself away from the girls just yet. I'm having way too much fun.

Kayla tries on some clothes and we all stand around outside the fitting room telling her how good she looks. Which is true. When she puts on a tight, red-and-black striped bodysuit tucked into a pair of beltless, wide-hipped blue jeans, she looks like she could be nineteen years old. The salesgirl tells her she should consider a modelling career. Kayla answers that her mother has already set up a portfolio shoot for her next month. I have to admit I'm impressed.

After the girls help me pick out some cleats, we stop at the Beautique Boutique, a cosmetics stand in the centre of one of the mall corridors. The girls urge me to sit for a makeover and I finally agree. The woman in charge is kind of reluctant to work on me but she has no other customers and I show her that I have the ten dollars needed to pay for the makeover. She starts powdering my face and applying makeup. She reminds me of a painter working on a canvas, only in this case my face is the canvas. When she's done, I look in the mirror and see a whole new Lizzie Lucas. I try not to think about the fact that my parents have a specific policy about makeup: I'm not supposed to wear any until I'm sixteen. The makeup brings out my cheekbones and rounds out my eyes. Personally, I think I could pass for sixteen years old. Too bad I'll have to wash it all off before I get home.

"You look great!" Natalie coos.

"A real stunner!" Jasmine agrees.

"Not bad for a rookie," Kayla concedes.

While I'm sitting there admiring my new face, all of a sudden I realize I've been at the mall almost an hour and I still haven't called my parents. I don't want the girls to think I'm a nerd, so I lie and say I have to use the washroom. Meanwhile, I race upstairs on the escalator, weaving my way through two old ladies loaded up with shopping bags, to the second level, where Neena's father's jewelry store is.

"Hi, Mr. Raman," I call, entering the store. I rest my body against a glass counter filled with watches and catch my breath. "Where's Neena?"

"She said she was going to the food court for a snack," Mr. Raman reports. He's busily repairing a gold watch band with a sharp blade that could pass for a surgical instrument, so he doesn't notice the makeup. I'm sure he'd be shocked by it.

"Mind if I call my parents to tell them I'm here?" I ask.

"Of course not." Mr. Raman looks up and smiles. I cover my face with my hand. "Please say hello to them for me."

I nervously punch the numbers to my place. I know I'm probably in for trouble. Mom answers. She asks me what's taken me so long to call and I make up a story about the bus breaking down. By the tone of her voice I'm not sure she believes me, but she doesn't hassle me. I'm just lucky she can't see my face. Then I'd really be in trouble. I'd be dragged out of that mall by her personally and grounded until sometime well into the twenty-first century.

I make my way down to the food court. Neena is nowhere in sight. I really want to get back to the girls, but at the same time I'd like Neena to join us. Hanging out with the cool crowd doesn't mean much unless Neena's there to share it with me. I mean, it was her idea in the first place for us to play soccer.

I decide to look around for her, poking my head into some of her favourite stores. Like Music Den, where Neena likes to spend time listening to the latest CDs on earphones plugged into the wall. But I don't find her. Same goes for Pets Are Us. As far as I can figure, Neena has disappeared.

I start back for Fashion Planet, where I said I'd meet Natalie, Jasmine and Kayla. I'm hoping they're still in there, trying on outfits.

Just then, out of the corner of my eye, I catch sight of Enzo. He's in Collectors Corner stocking up on the latest series of baseball cards. Maybe he's bumped into Neena, I think.

"Enzo, you seen Neena?" I ask.

He tears his eyes from his cards at the sound of my voice. "Hi Lizzie, how you doing?"

I told you he was a nice guy.

"I'm fine," I answer. "But I can't find Neena. You haven't seen her by any chance?"

"Actually, I have," Enzo replies. "She was in the arcade just a few minutes ago."

"The arcade?" Neena and I hardly ever hang out there.

"Yeah. She was with Justin and a few of the other guys from the team."

I manage a quick thank you and sprint to the arcade. Now I really want to get to the bottom of this. What's Neena doing with Justin and the boys from the soccer team?

I spot Neena right away. She and Justin are playing Alienoid together, teasing each other and laughing out loud. They look to me like they're having the greatest time. Maybe Justin really does like Neena, I think. Talk about everything finally falling into place!

"Neena!" I shout. "I've been looking all over for you!"

Neena wheels around to face me. Her face is flushed and her eyes are brilliant.

"Lizzie!" She's as excited as I am, rushing over to me. "What a day! What a day!"

"I can see that," I whisper. Justin is still playing Alienoid, but I can tell he's trying to listen in on our conversation at the same time. "You're making progress."

"You better believe it!" Neena pants. "Justin told me he likes me! Me!"

"No way!"

"Yes!"

Neena's long black hair bounces as she takes a series of tiny hops.

"Tell me more!" I demand. I'm so happy for her.

"I can't right now. We still have six quarters left to play Alienoid with. I'll meet you later at my dad's store and give you all the details. And you can tell me all about how you got that gorgeous new face!"

"For sure," I say. "I'll tell you all about my afternoon — shopping with Natalie, Jasmine and Kayla!"

"I think we've finally made it, Lizzie!"

"We're in the cool crowd now!" I gasp.

10

Whose Team Are We On, Anyway?

Take a good look around," Neena tells me as we step onto the soccer field for our first game with the boys' team.

We're playing against the Crescentwood Panthers, on their field, and fans are everywhere. Boys and girls from both schools mill behind the nets, dispensing advice to the players. Teachers and parents line the sidelines. I even spot Mr. Murray and Coach Laughton stepping out of a car and striding to the field.

"Are all these people here to watch us?" I ask.

"You bet," Neena replies.

That alone makes me nervous enough. But I'm even more nervous about how the boys on our team are going to treat us. Our first real practice together was sure upsetting. Now, if we're going to win the game ahead of us, we have to cooperate, play together like a team. Problem is, I'm not sure that's possible.

During the warm-up, the girls keep to one side of our team's end of the field, the boys to the other. Neena and I warm up together, as if we can somehow work away our nervousness just by being near each other.

I take a long look across the field. The green grass seems to slope down from the centre towards the sidelines. Strips of bright white paint mark the penalty and goal areas and the out of bounds. Red netting is fastened to the goals. Yellow banners are pegged into the ground at the corners. I'm actually excited about playing soccer today.

I also feel pretty good in my new cleats and the Corydon Eagles uniform, which I wear with the orange jersey tucked neatly into my shiny blue shorts. The red captain's armband is around my right bicep. I'm a real soccer player now.

Coach Borowski blows his whistle. "Come on in, team," he yells. Boys and girls form a half-circle in front of him. As we wait for his commands, a lot of us continue warming up, twisting our feet, shaking our legs, stretching our arms up into the air. I help Neena weave her hair into a tighter braid.

"I want all of you to listen to my advice carefully," Coach begins. "We're going to keep things simple today. Nothing fancy. I want to see a lot of passing out there. Help one another out. We're not here necessarily to win the game. We're here to learn what skills we still need to work on in order to mould this team into shape. You'll find the names and positions of the starting lineup listed on my clipboard, at the end of our bench."

First thing I do is grab a soccer ball from the equipment bag. Finding out if and where I'm starting can wait. Dad always says that a soccer player has to get comfortable with the ball. To feel like you and the ball are one. To know in what direction it'll travel if you kick it just so and what kind of bounces it takes on the grass.

I hold the ball between my hands and twirl it around in front of me. I let the ball bounce gently off my head, across the back of my shoulders and neck, down my back, off my thighs and knees, off my feet. I smell the ball, detecting not only the smell of leather but also of grass and dirt. Then I let the ball fall to the ground and nudge it from foot to foot, once in a while pushing it forward a bit, or up into the air a few centimetres. Finally, I give the ball a few good kicks.

I decide to check the starting lineup. As it turns out, all the girls are starting, except for Natalie, who will follow Victor in net for the second half. The paper on Coach's clipboard reads something like this:

Forwards: Enzo, Brad, Justin, Lizzie, Melanie
Halfbacks: Neena, Tyler, Frank
Fullbacks: Tony, Jasmine
Goalie: Victor

"Don't get too far from me out there, I'm going to need all the help I can get," Neena tells me as we begin passing a ball between us. She wears her jersey loose, outside her shorts, but in a way that doesn't look sloppy.

"So will I," I say. "So will I."

Finally, the referee blows his whistle and calls two players from each team to the centre circle. Coach sends me and Victor. I feel weird alone in the middle of the field with only Victor, the two Panthers captains, and the referee. I know all eyes must be on me, waiting for me to flub up. The referee asks me to call the coin toss. I call heads.

"Heads it is," the referee announces. I take a deep sigh of relief. "The Eagles will put the ball into play."

All the rest of the players run onto the field and take their positions. I look across the centre line at the player I have to cover. He's a short guy with thick, muscular legs that look like they belong to a horse. I begin to worry if I'll be able to keep up with him.

Justin starts the game by tapping the ball to Brad, who leads a pass over to Enzo a few metres into the opposing end. My legs suddenly feel like jelly and I have a hard time moving forward to keep up with the movement of the ball. My mind has gone blank, and I have absolutely no idea what I'm supposed to do.

Only seconds into the game and already I've lost focus.

In the next moment there's a mad scramble for the ball right in front of me. A half dozen pairs of legs are all struggling to gain control of the ball. Somehow the ball gets budged to me. I immediately give it a boot and send the ball flying deep into the Panthers end.

"Way to move the ball up!" Coach calls out.

I race after the ball. Making contact like that has wakened me up. Justin reaches the ball first and pulls a deke and dribble on the player marking him. He approaches the net. The Panthers goalie creeps towards Justin. Melanie has moved to Justin's right, apparently open, and Brad is right behind her.

Justin bears down to take a shot. The goalie dives at his feet. The ball bullets into the goalie and bounces back to Melanie. By this time a few Panthers defenders have backed up their fallen goalie and are blocking the net. Enzo, Brad and I are lurking around Melanie, waiting for her to make a move.

In the next instant Melanie nudges the ball to her side with the outside of her foot and lines up for a shot. If she puts enough power into her shot, she just might be able to break the Panthers' blockade.

As Melanie brings her leg back to swing into the ball, Brad suddenly lurches forward and steals the ball from her. She kicks into thin air, slipping onto the grass by the force of her forward momentum. Brad dribbles forward.

But the Panthers' fullbacks have abandoned their defensive postures and are charging Brad. One of them prods the ball loose from Brad's feet and clears the ball far into midfield. Brad looks around him, stunned. So much for cooperation.

Meanwhile, our forwards, including myself, are caught far in the opposing end. One of their midfielders snares the ball and passes it farther into our end. We're racing back to help with the defence, but we're still way behind the play. The Panthers' passing is fast and efficient. They're playing "connect the dots" on this soccer field. Before we know it, the ball's on the feet of their centre-forward and he kicks it high in the right corner of the net. Victor is left hanging in the air as the ball swooshes into the red netting.

Crescentwood 1, Corydon 0.

In no time, the Panthers are threatening again. Their left forward has swept wide with the ball and loops a beautiful, high crossing pass in front of our net. Another Panthers striker is lined up behind me awaiting the pass. In the last instant I propel myself straight up and meet the ball with my head. I push my forehead into the ball and pull my arms back for leverage. The ball goes soaring to Enzo, who works it slowly into the opposing end, close to the out-of-bounds line. I follow in pursuit. Once again, my heading ability has come in handy.

Tyler is steps ahead of Enzo and calls for a pass. Enzo sends a strategic pass through the legs of a Panthers defender and right to Tyler. Justin clears right to give Tyler room and make himself open, taking another Panthers defender with him.

By this time I've reached the line of assault and call out to Tyler that I'm open. This is a two-on-one situation for us. If he just passes to me the way we practised, we could create a neat give-and-go play here. He'd pass to me and I'd pass right back to him as he moves behind the Panthers fullback. I see it all clearly in my mind's eye.

I call out to Tyler again. He keeps his player at bay with some fancy moves but more Panthers defenders are on their way now. I know he sees me because our eyes meet.

But he decides to keep the ball. He dribbles around his marker, but by the time he's freed up in front of the net and in position to shoot, he's thoroughly pooped. His shot is weak and ineffective. The Panthers goalie gathers it up like a lost puppy.

The rest of the first half is more of the same. Our team just can't manage to put any kind of offence together. The boys aren't passing to the girls, and, before long the girls aren't passing to the boys. Meanwhile, the Panthers open up gaps in our defence with their precision passing. They're not more talented than us, just more organized.

When the whistle blows to signal half time, the score is Crescentwood 4, Corydon 0.

In the second half I get all of one opportunity to show my skills once more as a header. Our side has earned a corner kick. Coach Borowski assigns Melanie to take it. She stands alone at the corner to the right of the net and everybody else scrums in front of the net, waiting for the ball to come their way.

"Why are you letting her take the corner kick?" Brad complains to Coach Borowski. "She probably won't even be able to reach us."

Of course, Brad is all wrong. And he should know better because Melanie has already proven how good she is at soccer. She takes a running start and angles into the ball, her leg following through to give as much gumption to the kick as possible.

The ball's sailing right at me. I follow its arc through the air and set myself up to head it. I bounce on my feet and prepare to launch my head right into it.

But I feel a sudden jabbing in my ribs. Tyler has just given me a quick elbow poke, the same way he did in practice. The pain sure does feel familiar.

I tumble to the ground and the ball continues its flight. I see Justin lift his body to reach it. His head is straining to connect with the ball. But I notice that his eyes are closed. As the ball makes contact with his head, he flinches and pulls away from it, like he's afraid. The ball bops off the top of his head and flops harmlessly to the ground, where a Panthers defender reaches it and clears it out of their end.

I'm sure I could have headed that ball into the net. But I never did get the chance.

By the end of the game the score is Crescentwood 7, Corydon 0.

The way I see it, the only consolation is that our team let fewer goals in with Natalie in net, than we did with Victor there. I can't help thinking that there were three teams out there today. Crescentwood, the Corydon boys and the Corydon girls. That's no way to play soccer.

11

The Challenge

The Eagles step groggily onto the school bus that's waiting to take us back to Corydon Junior High, our heads hanging and our mouths silent. As a team, we've played terribly, and we feel awful. We take our seats and stare blankly out the bus windows.

The girls are sitting at the front left side of the bus, behind the driver's seat. None of the boys takes a seat beside us. Instead, they all spread out as far away from us as possible.

Coach takes a head count and then signals for the driver to take off. The driver shoves the long stick-shift into gear and the bus heaves forward. He leans over the huge steering wheel and directs the bus into a turn. I feel myself shoved into Neena, who's sitting beside me. Somehow I feel good just making physical contact with someone, especially someone friendly.

"That couldn't have gone any worse," I say. "I don't think there's much hope for this team."

Natalie, in the seat ahead of us, has overheard my comment and turns to face us. "Not if the boys don't change their tune."

"I don't think they will," Jasmine, who's sitting beside Natalie, puts in. Her hair is flat and stringy from all the sweating she's done. "I know these boys. They're stubborn."

"I'm not so sure," Neena says then. "Some of them are really coming around. Look at that nice pass Enzo made to Melanie. And how about that time Justin helped me up after I'd been tackled to the ground by their fullback?"

"Give us a break, Neena," Jasmine says. "You've got a crush on Justin and so you see everything he does with rose-coloured glasses. I'm telling you, it's like Kayla told me, he's just teasing you."

Neena is flabbergasted, her eyes ablaze.

"Teasing me!" she shouts. "What do you mean?"

Jasmine pauses a moment, her face held in hard concentration, as if she's considering whether or not she should explain her accusation.

"I don't know," she begins, "but Kayla says Justin is probably being nice to you as a kind of practical joke, the same way the boys chose Lizzie as team captain. He's setting you up for a bad fall. Sometime soon, he and the boys will share a good laugh at your expense."

"I don't believe that!" Neena protests. She twists her head to seek out Justin's face at the rear of the bus. But just at that moment he happens to be laughing uproariously with some of the boys, as if confirming Jasmine's words.

"Face it," Jasmine continues, "Justin Hope could go out with any girl in our school."

I see Neena working back her anger. Her cheeks flush. She glances towards me, seeking my help, but I don't know what to say. As far as I know, maybe Kayla and Jasmine are right and Justin is just teasing Neena, having his fun, the same way all the boys did with me, choosing me captain of the team.

"You never know," I say. I realize my statement can be taken either way, but I let it stand. I don't want Neena upset with me, but at the same time I don't want the other girls thinking I'm still a nerd with her head in the clouds.

The bus takes the turn into the school lot. As we all grab our gym bags and prepare to get off the bus, Coach speaks up.

"I can't let you go without letting you all know how poorly you played today. Soccer is a team sport and most of you ignored that fact. If we're going to win any games this season, we're going to have to learn to play together as a team."

The doors of the bus swing open with a rattle. Coach turns around to leave. But nobody else on the bus follows.

"This is a boys' team. The girls are just in the way," Victor hollers from the back of the bus.

"Yeah, how do you expect us to play with half-rate players?"

"The other teams are even making fun of us, saying we should all be wearing skirts."

"In sports, girls and boys just don't mix."

Coach turns back.

"The girls are here to stay and that's it," he declares.

"But they lost the game for us today," Brad pleads.

"They're losers!"

"They stink!"

That's too much. A person can only take so much abuse and then they just boil over. Like me just then. The boys are ripping us apart with no reason. This has just got to stop.

Once again, I open my mouth. Without thinking, but just reacting.

"If you boys think you're so much better than us girls, prove it. How about we challenge you to a Soccer Showdown. The five girls against your top five players." I'm standing now, leaning over the back of my seat, staring right at the boys. "If you win, we quit. We'll be out of your way forever more. But if we win, you boys have to shut your mouths and accept us on the team, no questions asked."

The boys are silent.

"You don't have to do this girls," Coach cuts in. "I'm guaranteeing you each a spot on this team for the rest of the season. You deserve it."

"No, we want to do this," a voice behind me declares. The voice is sharp and direct. "We can beat the boys."

I turn my head and realize that those words just came out of Melanie's mouth. I smile at her and I'm sure I detect something of an answering smile on her face.

"Well," I go on, "do you boys have the guts to accept our challenge?"

"You're on!" Victor cries.

"This'll be a piece of cake!" Brad yelps.

Coach shakes his head. "I'm not sure this is such a good idea," he offers.

"We are," I shout.

The other girls raise up a chorus of "Yeahs!"

"So are we," Victor proclaims.

"If you really want to do this," Coach continues, "then I suppose it's best if you do it under the school's supervision. You can play a week from today on the half-size field at Elm Elementary, and I'll arrange for referees."

"We'll be there," all five of us girls shout.

"So will we," Brad barks.

We storm out of the bus and into the sunshine. The girls high-five me. Neena smiles. "Just how many bright ideas do you have stored up in that head of yours?" she asks.

"Plenty," I answer, laughing. But the laughter's as much nervous as it is joyful. Are the girls really good enough to beat the boys in a Soccer Showdown?

12

School Hero, Part One

"L izzie, Lizzie, how about an interview?"

I'm not sure I've heard correctly. It's the day after our disastrous game and I'm walking to my locker to take out the books for my first class. My muscles are sore and I'd prefer to just coast through my classes as uneventfully as possible. The voice chasing me down is Belinda MacArthur's. She's the editor of the *Corydon Chronicle*, the school newspaper, which comes out once a month.

Oh no, I realize suddenly, she wants to talk to me, as captain, about how poorly our soccer team played yesterday afternoon. What am I supposed to say? Right now I'd rather not think about soccer.

Belinda steers me into a corner beside a water fountain and stands in front of me so I can't escape. She's holding a steno pad tilted at an angle in front of her, her pen poised on a clean sheet of paper ready to record my words.

"My sources tell me," she blurts out, "that you've challenged the boys on your team to a Soccer Showdown."

I'm speechless.

Belinda continues. "We at the *Corydon Chronicle* believe it's high time that school sports were organized on a more equitable basis, regardless of gender. I've written several editorials to that effect. We consider your efforts on behalf of the females in this school to be quite courageous. I'd like your comments, please."

Belinda only talks like that, all official-sounding and with big words, when she's on newspaper business. Normally, she's a pretty regular girl. But she does take her job as editor seriously. So seriously in fact that you just know she'll make it in journalism one day.

"Well ..." I falter. "What do you want to know?" I'm not used to being interviewed by Belinda, even though it does kind of sound like she's on my side. In fact, I'm not even used to being talked to by her. Until today, I'd hazard a guess that she didn't even know I existed.

"First of all," Belinda demands, "could you tell me why you issued the challenge to the boys?"

"On the record?" I ask. I'm kind of afraid to say anything negative about the boys. Part of me thinks maybe I've already made too many waves.

"Of course," Belinda replies, her face intent. "You're big news now, Lizzie Lucas. Everyone wants to know the details about the upcoming Soccer Showdown. Why? Where? When? What?"

By then a few students have noticed Belinda and me and gather around us to hear the interview. So much for the uneventful day at school I had planned.

"Your challenge serves as an inspiration to the females of this school," Belinda gushes. "Let me repeat my first question. Why'd you issue the challenge?"

Belinda's encouraging words embolden me. Suddenly I feel comfortable with my role as spokesperson for the five girls on the boys' soccer team.

"I issued the challenge," I begin, loud enough so that not only Belinda but all the other students bunched around us can hear, "because I didn't think the boys on the soccer team were treating the girls fairly. We just want to be able to play on their team, and they're doing all they can to prevent us from that opportunity. They weren't passing to us, and they were blaming all the team's mistakes on us. Something or someone had to give. I decided that if the boys think they're so good, they'd agree to a game against us. They have, and now the girls have a chance to prove they deserve their spots on the boys' soccer team. If we win, the boys accept us on the team with a whole new attitude. If we lose, we'll say goodbye and the boys' soccer team will never hear from us again."

The girls around us cheer. I hear one girl shout, "Way to go, Lizzie!" Another girl yells, "Equal opportunity soccer at Corydon Junior High, it's about time!"

The whole scene might as well be one of the little fantasies I used to have some nights when I couldn't sleep on account of someone or other making fun of me at school that day. I'd dream I was suddenly the most popular girl at school, everybody wanting to hang around with me, everybody listening to what I had to say. Now it's all coming true. I can't believe it. But this is no dream!

As the interview continues, more students assemble, especially girls. The few boys that are there try to defend their friends on the soccer team, but the girls drown them out with their loud cheers.

Even the school president, Faith Mulhaney, shows up. She's as excited about the Soccer Showdown as Belinda. She shakes my hand and whispers in my ear that she's supporting me all the way down the line on this issue.

Even the grade nines are talking to me now! This is too good to be true!

When Belinda asks for her comments, Faith says that if the boys don't back down and unconditionally accept the girls on their team, she's going to ask all the girls in the school to boycott the next school dance.

"The boys can go to the next dance alone, if they like," she declares. "If they think girls aren't good enough for the soccer team, then I guess we're not good enough to join them at dances, either."

All the girls send up a cheer. "Boycott the boys!" I hear several of them shout fervently.

The boys in the crowd jeer and boo. But I can tell some of them are nervous. I don't think they like the idea of a school full of uncooperative girls.

Finally, Belinda flaps her steno pad shut and shoves her pen into her back pocket. "This is the hottest news of the school year," she enthuses, running off towards the newspaper office, which is just a tiny room in the back of the art class. "I can't wait to write it up."

The girls who have gathered to support the Soccer Showdown take on the features of a mob. We march down the hallway together, chanting "Soccer Showdown! Soccer Showdown!" Teachers open their doors and peer at us. Most of them are excited about what we're doing.

Suddenly everybody wants to help our cause. One girl promises to paint a banner advertising the game. Another wants to take a picture of me for the school yearbook. If my junior high career's going to be like this, I decide, I never want it to end.

Just then, around the corner comes Neena, shoving her way through the throng of excited girls and clutching me by the arm, as our loud procession moves down the hallway toward the school gym, where we plan to hang banners advertising the Soccer Showdown.

But her usually bright eyes are now waxy with concern and her face is lined with worry.

"Lizzie, we need to talk," she pleads into my ear.

Obviously, she's not here to help proclaim the Soccer Showdown. I suppose she's still uncertain about whether or not Justin really likes her, and wants my advice. I wish she'd just drop it already and concentrate on soccer.

At that moment, three of the girls at my side decide to show me some ideas for posters they've quickly drawn. In the process, Neena is bumped away and falls behind the procession.

"Later, Neena," I call out to her, as the girls hold up my arms like those of a boxer who's just won a match.

I'm a school hero now.

13

School Hero, Part Two

Over the next few days, Corydon Junior High becomes a whole new school for me.

All of a sudden, as I move from class to class, everybody greets me. And knows my name.

"Hi, Liz!"

"How ya doin, Liz?"

"What's up, Liz?"

Everybody, that is, except the boys. Because ever since Belinda's fiery article appeared in the *Corydon Chronicle*, condemning the boys and praising the girls, myself in particular, the boys and the girls in our school haven't been talking to each other. It's an all-out cold war that promises not to be resolved until the Soccer Showdown is over and done with.

Still, I feel the boys' eyes upon me, noticing me for the first time, taking stock of me, trying to figure out what kind of girl could start all this fuss, which has even reached the point where a lot of girlfriends and boyfriends have vowed to shun each other until this matter is completely settled. I may not have the boys' friendship just yet, but I do have their respect.

The hallway walls are plastered with posters trumpeting the Soccer Showdown. All the teachers are talking about it in class. And Mr. Murray announces the Soccer Showdown's time and place over the intercom with his other morning announcements.

In Ms. Bernstein's History class we spend the whole thirty minutes discussing the Soccer Showdown as if it's actually part of our study program. She frames our discussion with some historical facts about the Women's Movement in North America, and then all of us just go at it. We end up having one of our liveliest classes ever, with everyone opening his or her mouth to offer opinions. It's fantastic!

Now my getting good marks doesn't make me geeky, but popular. It's as if the other students have decided that it's suddenly OK for me to be smart, now that I'm one of them. Several girls who used to ignore me have asked me over to their houses to help them study.

To be honest, part of me is having trouble keeping up with this new picture, as if this new Lizzie Lucas is someone somehow apart from me, even though, at the same time, it's also who I've yearned to be all along, the person I knew was lurking behind the cage all my classmates had constructed around me.

It's weird, isn't it?

I mean, finding out who you really are, what you *mean*, to yourself and to the people around you.

Amidst all this fervour and excitement over the upcoming Soccer Showdown, Melanie, Jasmine, Natalie, Neena and I do find an opportunity to hone our soccer skills and prepare for the game against the boys. We're lucky that my dad has offered his services on our behalf, and he takes us out to the smaller Elm Elementary soccer field to practise.

He leads us through all the basic drills and then introduces us to some advanced techniques. For example, he teaches Melanie how to use her heel to make totally unexpected passes and Natalie how to use her fists to deflect the ball away from the net. He has us work a few set plays as well, like the give-and-go, and instructs us on the proper positioning for a corner kick or a direct foul kick.

At the end of the practice, he makes us shoot penalty kicks on Natalie. A lot of games, he says, are won on a penalty kick, and he'd like all of us to be able to shoot smartly and for Natalie to know how best to stop a penalty kick. We work long and hard on these penalty kicks, and before long it's difficult to see who's improved more, the shooters, or Natalie in net.

When we're finally done, we're exhausted, and Natalie suggests we walk over to the corner convenience store for some pop. After his required pep talk about the courage against adversity shown by the Trojan Women, Dad takes off for home, and the five of us trudge across the field and down the street. Along the way we keep telling one another how we're going to beat the boys. There's a real feeling of camaraderie between us. We've all become best buddies. It feels good, it really does, to be a part of this group.

At the same time, I sense that something is wrong with Neena. I just can't understand what's going on. I mean, here we are finally fully involved with something exciting and she's moping around like we're still geeks. She's not even talking to me much, not like we're best friends, at least, but just as one teammate to another. I don't get it. I'm beginning to think that maybe she's a little jealous that I'm the one receiving most of the attention right now.

As we enter the convenience store, we spot a bunch of boys from the soccer team playing video games and reading comic books in the far corner. Justin is among them, and as soon as Neena sees him, she brightens. There she is, I think, still pining over Justin when we have serious business to take care of.

The girls pass the boys on our way to the stand-up coolers at the rear of the store and we make a big show of ignoring them. This is a cold war, remember.

However, Neena stalls a moment and makes eye contact with Justin. Jasmine grabs her by the arm to carry her forward but Neena breaks free and approaches Justin. Gosh, that girl has nerve.

"Hi, Justin. How you doing? Need someone to play Solar Shift with?"

My eyes are on Justin. I'm really curious to see how he'll react.

"Hi, Neena." Justin smiles and his blue eyes twinkle.

Jasmine cuts in then.

"Forget about it, Neena. We're not talking to the boys, *remember*?" She emphasizes that last word hard, like a scolding parent.

Melanie and Natalie open the cooler. "Come on, Neena, let's just get our drinks and get out of here," Natalie appeals.

"We don't need to see these boys until it's time for the Soccer Showdown," Melanie adds.

Neena refuses to be fazed.

"I'd like to spend some time with Justin, if that's OK with you" — she faces Jasmine — "and the rest of the team" — she stares down Natalie and Melanie.

"Grab a brain," Jasmine continues. "Justin's just teasing you." Then Jasmine turns to me. "Tell her, Lizzie, she's your friend."

At that point, as I see it, I have two choices. I could stand up for Neena, my best friend, and risk bursting my balloon of popularity, or I could side with Jasmine and the girls and bolster my reputation as a school hero even more.

Unfortunately, I make the wrong decision. And I know I do even as I'm doing it. But I still do it.

"You're a traitor Neena," I call out. I can't believe I've just said those words. Against my better judgement, I'm playing follow-the-leader even worse than Jasmine.

Neena looks at me with a bewildered expression weighing upon her face. I can tell she's too shocked to say a word.

Jasmine breaks the silence. "Justin doesn't like you, Neena. He's taking you for a ride."

I see the flame of firm denial in Justin's eyes and know then that he truly likes Neena. I don't know much about romance, but I think I do know enough to tell when a boy really likes a girl. Justin likes Neena. Really.

In that instant Justin reaches into his pocket and pulls out a handful of quarters.

"Help me finish these off, will you Neena?" he says.

Neena smiles. "Sure thing." She faces me defiantly, but I don't have the courage to look her in the eyes. I drop my gaze and stare blankly at the floor. Then I lift my head again, trying to say something, although I'm not sure what. But Neena and Justin have moved over to the Solar Shift monitor and begun playing, close together so that they're almost touching.

Jasmine offers me a perplexed face. Even the boys don't know what to make of Justin's behaviour. But I do. Unlike me, he's being a good friend to Neena.

I expected Neena to be happy for me and my new popularity, but now, as her best friend, I couldn't show her that I was happy for her new popularity, with Justin. Maybe I was jealous. I don't know.

"You had to tell Neena off like that," Jasmine says, as we reach into the cooler for our drinks. "You did the right thing."

Natalie and Melanie hang back by the counter, unconvinced.

I grab an orange soda and push it against my cheek to cool myself. I'm sweating with discomfort. This is a new Lizzie Lucas, all right. And right now I don't like her at all.

"Let's get out of here," I say.

14

Soccer Showdown

As far as I can tell, the entire school has shown up for our Soccer Showdown. Every centimetre of sideline at the Elm Elementary field is lined with fans. Students, teachers, parents, friends. Perry, Sia and my mom are there, too. Neena's parents are beside them, her mom wearing a bright orange sari. All of them are jumping up and down, rooting us on.

As for Dad, he's stalking the sidelines, calling out instructions.

"Put more leg power into those shots! Don't forget to play the ball, not the man! Control the ball, and you control the game!"

I get the feeling he wishes he could be out on the field playing for our side.

Bending down, I tighten my shoelaces and pull up my socks. All of a sudden, an action as simple as that somehow takes on immense importance. I do it very carefully, tying the shoelaces just so and making sure my socks are pulled evenly, with no bunching. Everything has to be done right. I don't want to jinx myself.

Melanie, Jasmine and Neena are taking practice shots on Natalie, who seems to be in fine form, gliding to her right and left to make the saves. That's good. We'll need excellent goalkeeping to win this game. I take my place in line and begin to take some shots of my own. The mere act of kicking the ball helps loosen me up. To tell the truth, I'm so thrilled to be playing today there's really no time for nervousness.

The five boys opposite us are Victor, who's keeping goal, Tyler and Enzo in the middle, and Brad and Justin up front. There are two referees sharing the officiating duties, Mr. Cuthbertson and Miss Shaw. Remember, this game is supposed to be played as fairly as possible.

One factor nobody was counting on is the weather. Throughout the whole day dark clouds have been gathering in the sky, in all sorts of monstrous shapes, like there's some sort of dark cloud meeting going on.

I wish I could say something to Neena to make things better, but I don't want to start things off again and tear a deeper rift into the team. Part of me wishes she hadn't put me in the position to be mean to her in the first place. If she'd only stopped mooning over Justin after practice the other day, we wouldn't be in this mess. Then again, I had no right to open my mouth and single her out. Truth is, Neena has put a lot of effort into practising her soccer skills. I was wrong. Period.

Somehow Melanie senses that my squabble with Neena has undercut my ability to perform effectively as team captain and she takes charge. I appreciate that. There are times, I suppose, when you just get kind of weak — whether it's your fault or not — and it's nice to have someone realize that and step in for you.

"One minute to starting time," Miss Shaw announces.

"Come on, girls," Melanie calls, "let's get the show on the road."

We form a tight circle in front of our net.

"We can win this game," Melanie says. "If we just work hard and play smart." Her intensity is contagious.

"If we can control the ball, we can control the game," I put in, echoing Dad's advice.

"Right," Jasmine says. "Let's force the boys to make mistakes."

Natalie stretches out her arm, her hand at the end of it formed into a tight fist. All of us follow her lead, our hands on top of one another's over hers. Neena's hand happens to be the one beneath mine. The moment I feel Neena's skin against mine I feel even worse about the way I treated her. I don't have the words just then to tell her I'm sorry, so I try to hold her hand in a way that she'll get the message. Tight. And warm. I'm hoping she'll forgive me.

"One, two, three, go team!" we shout in unison. The sound of all our voices melded together makes my heart pound faster. The adrenaline races through my blood. I'm pumped. I feel as if I'm part of some sort of comic book superhero team.

As we take our positions on the field, I can tell the boys are nervous, because they're moving around aimlessly in tight little circles, waiting out the opening whistle. I have a feeling they're not as organized as we are. Once again I think how lucky we are to have my dad as coach.

In the next moment, the whistle blows. And the Soccer Showdown begins.

Immediately, the boys try to take charge by using their brawn. Justin taps the ball to Brad, who plows down the middle of the field. I charge him, but he steamrolls past me. There's no finesse to his drive, just pure muscle. Somehow he retains control of the ball. I'm left tripped up on the grass, thinking that if only I were a little stronger I might have been able to strip Brad of the ball.

Now in the open, Brad looks to his side for a fellow attacker and spots Justin breaking wide on the right. He loops a nice pass Justin's way and holds back to stay onside. Justin takes in the ball and runs forward a few paces, then hesitates a moment to scope the field for a crossing pass.

That gives Neena enough time to reach Justin. She lunges toward him, her right knee scraping the ground and her left foot extended outward. The ball is poked free. It's a textbook sliding tackle, but Neena is going to pay the price with a sore right leg. I should have known all along Neena was too much of a team player to treat Justin with kid gloves just because she happens to like him. I'm sorry I ever doubted her.

Now Neena bounces back to her feet and chases down the ball. When she reaches it, she knocks it forward to Melanie. Melanie controls the ball and boots it far and clear. We're safe.

But not for long. Once again the boys set up an attack. Tyler whacks Melanie's clearing shot back into our end. Enzo is there to nab it and presses forward. He passes to Brad, who's cutting towards the net. Brad picks up the ball and dekes around Jasmine. He's alone against Natalie. The space between them narrows as Brad barrels to the net. Natalie flings her body at Brad's feet. Still, he manages to get a shot away. The ball booms towards the goal. I hold my breath. And then THWACK! the ball hits the crossbar and bounces to my feet.

"That was too close for comfort, girls," my father cries out. "Slow down the pace! Control the ball!"

I take his advice. I dribble the ball slowly upfield, waiting for the other girls to set themselves up in their proper positions. The boys retreat, building their defence. I see Neena in the open and pass the ball her way. She traps it with the sole of her foot. I smile. Neena boots the ball to Jasmine. Jasmine knocks it back to Melanie. Melanie returns the ball to me. Metre by metre, we've reached past the centre line.

I notice the boys growing impatient. Brad decides to charge me. As he does so, Melanie smartly slips into the spot he's just vacated. I slide the ball to her. She traps it and moves forward. This time Tyler's nerves falter. He pounces on Melanie. Adroitly, she dribbles by him. Frustrated at being beaten, Tyler grabs Melanie's jersey and pulls her to the ground.

Mr. Cuthbertson blows his whistle. "Foul!" He sets the ball down outside the penalty crease for a free kick. "One more stunt like that, young man, and you're out of the game." I hear razzing coming from the crowd.

Jasmine sets up for the free kick, Melanie beside her, Neena wide to the right, myself wide to the left. Jasmine taps the ball to Melanie. Neena and I break for the net. Melanie brings her leg back and chips the ball high up in the air. I follow its arc and try to position myself to head it. Tyler gives me a shove to push me out of the way, but I just shove back. To be honest, I'm not too surprised or sorry when I see his rear end plunk down onto the ground.

At the same time, the ball begins its descent. I bound up on my legs and spring into the air. I follow the ball — each visible seam — with my eyes. I make contact with my forehead. I strain my neck and push the ball with all the force I can muster. Victor leaps to his right to make the save. As his torso touches the ground, the ball bounces in front of him and then over him. The ball bobs into the net.

A goal!

The girls jump on top of me. Even Natalie leaves her net and joins the pile-up. I can hardly breathe under all that weight. Even so, I feel wonderful. Most of all because I feel Neena's warm body next to mine, congratulating me along with the others.

The girls and women in the crowd go wild. So do a lot of the boys and men, like Neena's dad and my brother. And my dad, who's jumping up and down. "That's my daughter!" I hear him declare proudly to the two referees.

It's total mayhem. In the din, Enzo reaches out to tap me on the shoulder. "That was some goal," he says. "I'd like to see the replay."

Behind him, Victor's shaking his head for having missed the save. I can tell he's heard Enzo's comment and I wonder what he'll have to say. I wait. In a moment, he opens his mouth. "Good header, Lucas," he grumbles. "But we'll get that goal back."

I take his words as a compliment, and leave it at that. Who knows, maybe these boys will come around?

But even louder than the cheer over the goal is the sudden roar of thunder from the dark sky. It's like a thousand fire-crackers go off simultaneously. The clouds actually appear to shake from the rumble. We all look up, begging the rain off. Unfortunately, we might have been better off performing a rain dance. In no time, a drizzle begins spitting down on the field.

"Let's continue," Miss Shaw calls out. "It looks like we just might have to hurry if we want to complete this game."

As we regroup, Melanie reminds the team that there's still plenty of game left. "Let's keep on playing carefully," she says. "This game is far from over."

I look closely at her. In her face, I see something more than the determination that is usually drawn there. I see a spark, a kind of excitement. It's my guess that she's enjoying this game more than anything she's enjoyed in a long time.

For the rest of the half, we play a conservative, defensive game. The boys don't get too many worthwhile opportunities because the playing surface is getting steadily more wet and slippery. It's difficult just running around any more, let alone getting a good shot on net. Besides, we build a seamless wall as the boys enter our end of the field.

At the end of the half, our one-goal lead is still intact. The girls trot off the field, our heads held up high.

15

Second Half

By the time we run back to the centre line to begin the second half, the steady drizzle has transformed the playing field into a muddy bog. There are puddles everywhere, particularly a huge one right in front of the boys' net. You can hardly discern the out-of-bounds lines. The air is thick and sticky as fish soup. All of us will have a tough time moving about. This promises to be an entirely new game.

The boys, of course, want a goal badly and force the game to us. We try to hold ground, but they keep coming at us with aggressive rushes down the middle. First Brad. Then Tyler. Then Justin. Each of them gets through our defence and each of them lets loose a shot that, fortunately, is stopped by Natalie's sure hands.

"Let's tighten up out there!" Dad cries out. "The boys are bound to score if we keep handing them those shots."

We do our best. But the boys keep coming, and our counterattack never really gets off the ground. The kind of pinpoint passing we were pulling off in the first half is almost impossible in this mud. Passes trickle lamely into puddles. The ball is water-logged and heavy. The boys' superior strength is suddenly a critical factor.

Sure enough, about midway through the second half, Justin uses his power to jam the ball through Melanie's legs and make a run for the net. Neena tries to stop him but she slips on the muddy grass. Justin passes across to Brad. The ball moves slowly but finds its target. Brad one-times the ball on net. Natalie just barely reaches the ball with a dive and punches it back out into play. Justin is there for the rebound. So am I. I stretch out for the ball. My cleats lose their footing and I splatter into a puddle of mud. Justin takes the shot. The ball sails into the net, trailing a tail of dirty water.

The boys celebrate. Melanie, Neena, Jasmine and I console Natalie. She had no chance on that shot.

"There's more where that came from!" Brad jeers.

"We're waiting!" Melanie challenges back.

None of the fans have left the game. They're still all lined up on the sidelines, only now a few people have pulled out umbrellas and clusters of people take shelter under them. Others are wearing yellow slickers. Everyone's in a good mood. It's like a great big party out there.

On the field, it's another story. Our jerseys cling to our backs. Our hair is matted to our heads. Our bodies shiver from the mix of hot sweat and cool rain. The soaking rain and muddy field weighs us down. I'm so tired I'm ready to drop. Not to mention my allergies have kicked in and I'm sneezing all over the field.

But we have to struggle on. This game's still up for grabs, and the last thing we want right now is to allow the boys to run away with it.

I collect the ball and pass it to Jasmine. Jasmine spots Melanie and toes it to her. Near the out-of-bounds line, Melanie keeps the ball to herself and drives for the goal. Tyler moves in on her and sneaks out his right foot. Melanie goes flying.

No whistle is called. In the thick drizzle the referees are having a difficult time following the action.

Tyler steals the loose ball and smacks it up to Enzo. Enzo out-dribbles Jasmine and passes to Justin. As Melanie and I are caught behind the play, Justin enters the penalty area and stops. Beside him on one side is Enzo, on the other Brad. Neena is in front of him, marking him closely, with Jasmine next to her. He fakes to his left and makes for his right. Neena sticks to him like glue. With nowhere to turn, Justin passes to Enzo. Enzo lines up the ball and fires. Natalie reaches for it but falls short. The ball tents the netting as the boys throw up their arms to celebrate their second goal.

Suddenly, the boys lead the game, and there are only five minutes or so left in regulation time.

"I told you we had more goals coming!" Brad rubs in.

Dad calls a time-out. Some of our supporters hand us towels to wipe ourselves with. I feel people patting me on the back. I hear shouts of encouragement.

"We have to set up some sort of play," Dad commands. "I'd like to see a give-and-go situation, where Melanie passes the ball to one of you and then you feed it right back to her. That should leave Melanie in the open for a good shot."

"Got it!" we all call out.

"Good," Dad says. "No matter what happens in the next five minutes, girls, you've played fantastic soccer today, and you have everything to be proud of. Good luck."

We jog back onto the field. I put the ball into play by passing it to Neena. Quickly, she moves it to Jasmine, who crosses the ball to Melanie.

Instead of waiting for us to make the next move, the boys storm the ball. Brad reaches Melanie first and tries to mug the ball away from her. But she razzle-dazzles him by flipping the ball up into the air and juggling it over Brad's shoulder. He trips over himself and takes a seat in the mud. Once again, as in our first practice, Melanie's ball-juggling has put Brad to shame.

Then Melanie cuts to the middle. I follow, and position myself about fifteen metres from the goal. We could pull off a give-and-go now. Melanie slides the ball to me and slips forward. Without even moving I direct the ball into Melanie's path. She runs straight ahead, reaching the ball before any of the boys. She gives the ball a little tap with her foot to size it up and then lets loose a rocket of a shot. At the last second, Victor deflects the ball behind the net with an outstretched leg.

It's time for a corner kick. And probably our last chance to score a goal.

Melanie runs to the corner to take the kick. The rest of the players scramble in front of the net, jostling for position.

"Look out for Lizzie," Victor calls out to the rest of the boys.

It's not much, but I take his warning as another compliment to my heading abilities. In their own way, these boys surely are coming around.

Melanie sends the ball on a high arc. I feel elbows and shoulders nudging me and I just nudge back. I jump up to connect with the ball. But someone's right next to me. In the tight scrum I can't make out who it is, but I'm sure it's either Brad or Tyler. I eye the ball and lean into it. An elbow stabs my ribs. Still, I get my head on the ball. The ball bounces past Victor's outstretched hands into the top right corner of the net.

The game is tied!

I drop to the ground, my body swimming in the huge puddle in front of the boys' net. The girls and several fans swarm me. I'm soaking wet but loving every second of it. We've tied the boys in the Soccer Showdown. Now they'll have to accept us onto their team.

After a few more minutes of inconsequential play, the referees blow their whistles to signal the end of the game. We jump up and down and run across the mud-splattered field. We might as well have won, we feel so great.

The boys look dejected, but they still shake our hands and call out "good game," even Brad and Victor. Whether they're willing to admit it or not, we've earned their respect. The other players on the team console them. Girls from around the school congratulate us.

"I guess we're on the team for good!" Jasmine calls out.

"Who says?" Tyler spews. "The deal was if you won, we had to accept you on the team, but you didn't win."

"Yeah!" bellow a host of boys standing behind Tyler who are on the team but weren't playing in today's Soccer Showdown.

"The deal also was that if you won, we'd quit," Jasmine retorts. "You didn't, so we won't."

There's some shoving and it even looks like a fight might break out, as Justin and some of the other boys tell Tyler and his bunch to lay off us. But they're persistent.

"You didn't win," Tyler pouts. "Nothing changes."

"Come on, Tyler," Enzo cuts in, "the girls played well. They proved themselves."

"Yeah," Justin adds, "they just about beat us."

But Tyler and his cohorts won't be calmed.

"Maybe there should have been some other boys out there today," one of them says. "Maybe all of you guys weren't up to the job."

"Shut up!" Brad mutters. All the girls' eyes turn to him, considering he hasn't exactly been one of our biggest boosters. "I was there on the field today, and I side with Justin and Enzo. These girls are the real thing."

The boys who are against accepting us onto the team hiss and holler. "Traitors!" the boys shout.

"A deal's a deal," Tyler continues. "How can we let the girls onto the team if they didn't win, like they were supposed to?"

My dad approaches the fray just then. I can tell by the hard look on his face that he's heard a lot of the insults Tyler and his gang have been throwing around.

"There is a way for this to be settled," he announces.

We all look at him with startled expressions.

"How?"

"Penalty kicks," comes the reply. "That's the way we used to do it in the pro leagues. You take turns kicking penalty shots. First team that scores while the other team misses, wins the game."

Silence.

The girls share a secret glance. All that penalty-kicking practice with Dad just might come to some good after all.

Meanwhile, the boys confer with one another. Most of them are reluctant to continue the game. But Tyler is the loudest and he wants this thing to come to a conclusion, a conclusion he can live with.

Finally Tyler snarls, "You're on."

16

Penalty Kick

"Call it in the air," Mr. Cuthbertson says as he tosses a coin above his head.

"Heads," I call. I always stick with a winner.

The coin splats into a puddle of mud. Mr. Cuthbertson digs it out and shows it clearly in front of him. "Heads it is. The girls get to choose whether they'll shoot first or last."

"Last," I call immediately. That way we'll always have the last chance.

The players and refs trudge over to the far net where all the shots will be taken. The fans move accordingly along the sidelines. Meanwhile, the other girls and I try to boost Natalie's confidence and wish her our best as she takes her place in the net.

Justin is set as the boys' first shooter. He lines up the ball carefully and takes four precisely measured steps back. Poised on the goal line, Natalie bounces on the balls of her feet, feints with her shoulders, waiting for him to make contact with the ball, at which time she can start moving forward as well, cutting down his angle.

Justin takes a running start and connects. The ball bullets to the top right corner of the net.

Natalie propels her body upwards but can't reach the ball. It's a goal. The boys shout with joy.

Natalie shakes her head disconsolately and vacates the net for Victor.

Dad selects Melanie as our first shooter. We all cheer her on. The crowd goes wild with support.

She trots up to the ball and kicks in the exact opposite direction from where she was staring. Victor goes diving in one direction, the ball glides into the net in the other direction.

The rest of the girls clap our hands excitedly. We're still even with the boys.

Brad is the next shooter. I can tell he's nervous by the way he ignores the crowd and just stares at the ball. Finally, he begins his kick. He brings his leg back. But he tries to chip the ball and his foot goes too low and hits the grass before it connects with the ball. His shot trickles right into Natalie's hands.

All of us holler with excitement.

I'm next. If I score, we win the game. If I miss, we're still in it. There's as little pressure on me as there could be in a situation like this. Still, I'm nervous. At the same time, I'm excited. I sneak a peak at my dad and I can tell he's proud of me, supporting me.

I hold the ball in my hands and get comfortable with it, rubbing my hands along the seams and feeling the soaked leather. I wipe the wetness off my hands and onto my shorts. Then I set the ball neatly on the ground and ready myself for the shot. Victor is moving along the goal line trying to distract me. I do my best to ignore him. I make my move and swerve the ball high into the left corner. Victor dives, but his outstretched hands can't reach the ball. The ball continues its arc and appears to be sailing into the net. At the last second, though, it curves into the corner where the crossbar meets the goal post. The ball bounces harmlessly back to me.

The boys sigh with relief.

Enzo is the next shooter. He lines up and takes his crack at the ball. Natalie, expecting a powerful shot, overreacts and dives too far. The ball sneaks in behind her.

Once again, the girls are against the wall.

Neena's next. "Come on, Neena, you can do it," I call out. She looks at me and smiles. I'm forgiven, I'm sure. I feel almost as relieved about that as I would about winning this game. Without even realizing it, I find myself shouting, "I love you, Neena."

A few people in the crowd laugh. Neena gives me the thumbs-up sign back.

"Go for it!" Jasmine yells.

Neena runs up to the ball. She puts her instep into the ball and sends it travelling fast along the ground to the far left side, like a rabbit scurrying for a carrot. Victor throws out his legs, trying for a kick save. Just as the ball is about to cross the goal line, he nicks it with the toe of his cleat. The ball veers just wide of the net.

The boys go wild, jumping for joy. Even Justin and Enzo, but I have a feeling they're jumping not so much because they beat us but because they've just won what turned out to be a great game.

The girls hang their heads in shame. We really thought we could win this one. Nobody points a finger at Neena. She did her best. We all did. We're a team and we win and lose as a team.

"That was a great shot," Melanie says.

"Yeah," Jasmine echoes. "Way to play."

"Don't worry about it, Neena," I add.

The five of us embrace, forming a closed, tight circle, as the cold rain falls from the sky, the heat from our overtired bodies warming one another, happy that we're such good friends, sad that the soccer season for us is as good as over.

17

Friends through Thick and Thin

The next morning when my alarm goes off the last thing I feel like doing is getting out of bed and going to school. My body feels numb from all the work and wetness it endured during the Soccer Showdown. I've created a little cocoon for myself beneath the quilt and don't want to move. Why not ignore the whole world? I think to myself. Why not skip school? Who needs to go back now?

Something inside, though, pushes me slowly out of bed and into the shower, where the first blast of water succeeds in waking me up. I fix myself up as best I can and sit down for breakfast with Perry and Sia.

"Sorry about yesterday's game, Lizzie," Perry says, munching on a slice of toast. "If you ask me, you girls played way better than the boys."

"Thanks," I mumble, as I pour cereal into a bowl. "But we lost."

Sia is taking a last look at herself in the downstairs bathroom, but overhears my words. "You guys aren't going to give up now, are you?" she shouts. "You deserve your spots on that team."

I swallow a spoonful of cereal and begin my reply as Sia enters the kitchen. "It's not worth the trouble," I say. "We haven't discussed anything yet, but I think we'll have to quit. I mean, a deal's a deal. Besides, I'm not sure I'd want to play on the same team as those boys. A lot of them have a very poor attitude."

Sia takes a bite out of an apple, then shakes the bitten apple at me. "It's your job to change that attitude," she lectures.

"No," I say. "We've already tried everything there is to try. We did our best. We won't be playing any soccer this year."

Perry places two more slices of bread into the toaster (two slices are never enough for him). "If it's any consolation, Sis, watching you play yesterday really reawakened my interest in soccer. I say we have one of our family games sometime this week."

"Yeah," Sia echoes, smiling. "I think I'd like that, too."

"Thanks, guys," I say. "I'm sure that'll be nice. But I'll miss my teammates. We had a good thing going this year. You know, everybody at school knows my name now, on account of the Soccer Showdown. What'll happen now? Do I go back to being a geek?"

Sia makes a face. "I hate that word," she declares. "You're not and you never were and never will be a geek. Nobody is."

"Maybe I wasn't," I respond, "but most of my classmates thought I was. That's what counts. Frankly, I liked being popular."

"If you've made any real friends, they'll stick by you," Sia says. "And there's always Neena."

I chew the inside of my cheek to stifle a sob I feel breaking through my chest. I don't want to tell Sia or Perry about how I've treated Neena since the beginning of this whole Soccer Showdown fuss. Truth is, though, I can't say for sure how things will be now between Neena and me. I know I'm forgiven, but will we still be the same kind of friends? Best friends? I'm in a real mess.

At school later that morning, I search for Neena to patch things up with her once and for all, but I can't find her. I can tell she's at school, because she's taken some books out of the locker. I really want to find her before the nine o'clock bell rings because we don't have a class together until after lunch. I'm not sure I can wait that long with this heavy feeling on my chest.

In Math class, I sit behind Jasmine.

"I'm still steaming about that game yesterday," she confides as Mr. Brewster writes out an elaborate percentage problem on the blackboard.

"Tell me about it," I say. "I wish it had turned out differently; that would have served the boys right."

"I just don't think it's fair that they're getting away with this," Jasmine says. "We should be on that team, there's no two ways about it. If anything, that's exactly what yesterday's game proved."

"I know," I say, "but what are we supposed to do now?"

"I don't know," Jasmine ventures. "But somehow there should be a way to set this thing right. I just don't know how."

My mind's still on Neena.

"By the way," I ask, "have you see Neena around today? She wasn't at our locker this morning and I've been looking all over for her."

Jasmine shakes her head sadly. "You know something, Lizzie, I don't mind Neena now, I really don't, but I think she's overdoing it with her crush on Justin. Before class I saw her and Justin and some other boys hanging around together outside the principal's office. She was talking to them and everything. Isn't she mad about what happened yesterday, like us?"

"I haven't talked to her yet," I answer, "so I can't say." I know it's only right that I stick up for my best friend. "But I'm sure she feels as badly as we all do about the way the Soccer Showdown turned out."

"I hope so," Jasmine says. "I'm also kind of concerned about Melanie. She was really coming around with this soccer thing, and now it's pulled right from under her."

"This isn't right," I say, as much to myself as to Jasmine. "It just isn't."

The second class of the day is cancelled on account of Mr. Murray calling a surprise assembly in the gym for the whole school. Nobody knows what the assembly is about but rumour has it he's going to discuss the Soccer Showdown. Then again, another rumour has it that he's going to discuss some sort of new cross-country Math and English exam we'll all have to suffer through.

As I enter the gym, I scope around for Neena. I spot her sitting alone at the edge of the bleachers and head in that direction.

"Hey, Neena," I call before I reach her. "Care for some company?"

"Of course." She smiles and her sapphire eyes sparkle with warmth. "Have a seat."

"I heard Mr. Murray is going to bring up the Soccer Showdown," I say.

"So did I," Neena says. "And when he does, I think every-one's in for a big surprise."

"What do you mean?" I ask.

Neena gives me a mischievous grin and shooshes me with a finger brought against her lips. "Just wait and see," she commands.

Mr. Murray takes the podium and taps the microphone to make sure it's working. He gets the students' attention as an electric buzz echoes inside the gym walls.

"Ladies and gentlemen," he begins, in his steady, gentle voice, "we have several matters to consider today, so I'd like to get started as soon as possible."

The gym hushes and the only sound comes from a few students straightening out their metal fold-out chairs on the gym floor.

"First of all, there is the matter of the National Mathematics and Language Arts exam all of you, grades seven through nine, will be asked to write in the final week of school."

The students emit a collective groan.

"Every student your age in Canada has to write this exam, so there's no use complaining about it," Mr. Murray continues. "Indeed, it is my sincere hope that even though this exam is not worth any marks on your final grades..."

A sigh of relief travels through the gym like a wave.

"... all of you will put forth your best effort so that our school can come up with marks that truly reflect the skill level I know the students in this school are capable of achieving."

Some of the students begin talking amongst themselves.

"In any case," the principal persists, "your home-room teachers will be giving you more details about the contents of these tests. For now, I'm simply asking all of you to give the exam your best shot."

Mr. Murray coughs into his hand and adjusts the microphone closer to his lips.

"I would like also today to discuss the controversy that has shaken our school over the last few weeks concerning the five girls who attempted to earn a place on the boys' soccer team."

The gym goes silent. I look at Neena, brightening up. What could Mr. Murray be up to?

"I want to congratulate each of the five girls — Melanie Kline, Jasmine Hunt, Natalie Lundstrom, Neena Raman and

Lizzie Lucas — for a truly heroic effort. If the decision were up to me, I would hand them a spot on the boys' team this very second. Unfortunately, after lengthy conversations I've held this morning with Coach Borowski and Coach Laughton, as well as the student council, I have come to the conclusion that I will respect the arrangement agreed to by both the girls and the boys."

A few boys cheer the news, but most of the students in the gym hiss and boo.

"I come to this decision, regretfully, I must say," Mr. Murray adds, "for, I repeat, I think the boys are making a big mistake by not allowing these five girls to continue playing on their team. I was there watching the game yesterday, and I saw the girls play some wonderful soccer."

Just then Justin rises out of his chair and raises his arm. Mr. Murray doesn't notice him, because he's looking down at his notes. So Justin steps up on his chair and calls out, "Mr. Murray!"

Our principal is startled. I don't think he's ever been interrupted like this before at an assembly. He's the only one that does the talking at these things. But now he puts down his notes and looks directly at Justin.

"Yes, Justin, do you have something to say?"

Beside me, Neena is smiling.

"Well, sir," Justin begins, in that easy, confident tone of his, "some of us boys have been discussing what happened yesterday ourselves, and we've decided that we're going to quit the soccer team if the girls aren't allowed to play."

A round of applause fills the gym. And then Enzo stands up beside Justin, and a whole bunch of other players from the team who are sitting in different spots around the gym floor and in the bleachers also rise. I see Frank and Tony and even Brad and Victor.

"We're with Justin," Enzo proclaims for all of them.

I can't believe my eyes! Or my ears!

"You guys are all traitors," Tyler snorts, looking around him at the standing members of the team. "How could you do this? You heard Mr. Murray, we can have our way. We don't have to do this!"

"But we want to," Justin says. "It's only fair."

"Face it," Brad says, staring down Tyler. "We were wrong. Those girls *are* good enough to play on our team. They proved it."

Mr. Murray takes control once again before this disagreement gets too far out of hand. I can tell he's holding back a smile.

"In light of these new developments," he says, "I think that this whole issue is far from closed. I'm relieved to see that some of the boys have come to the proper decision without my pressure. Good for them. Perhaps there's still room for hope."

At that point, Ms. Bernstein speaks up. "Mr. Murray, could I make a suggestion?" she asks.

Teachers and students turn to face her.

"Because this matter has become a school issue, with all the students very much involved in the debate, could we perhaps settle the matter right here by letting the students — the whole school — vote on whether or not they'd like to see the girls allowed to play on the team?"

The gym rocks with agreement.

"Fine," Mr. Murray says. "I don't see why we can't settle the matter right now, with an old-fashioned vocal show of yeas and nays."

Tyler pipes up. "This isn't fair. The girls have already agreed to quit the team. And you said it was OK."

"That's right!" another boy shouts.

Something inside me starts ticking again, and I feel my face twitching and my stomach twirling. I just have to say something. I stand up on my chair and wave my hands.

"Yes, Lizzie?" Mr. Murray calls out.

I'm an expert at getting heard now. I close my eyes and take a deep breath. Then I open my eyes and take a look around at the students inside the gym. For the first time ever I see them not as parts of the cool crowd or the geeky crowd, but as individuals. I'm not scared of anyone any more. They're all kids, just like me. Including Tyler and his pals.

"Go for it," Neena whispers to me. "Come on, Lizzie, make me proud."

"We may have quit the team," I say, "but only because we didn't want to go back on our words. We love soccer, all five of us, and we're getting better at it every day. We tried hard, and I really think we deserved to make the team. I think Coach Borowski would agree with me on that, too. If the rest of the school wants us on the boys' team, I think I speak for the rest of the girls when I say we'll be glad to rejoin."

Neena starts applauding wildly, and Jasmine, Natalie and even Melanie join her.

Faith Mulhaney, sitting in the first row with the rest of the student council, rises to speak then. She addresses the principal, but turns to face the students behind her as well. She's a natural-born public speaker.

"As president of the student council, I know just how much extra attention boys' sports get over girls' sports. It's just not fair. I think these girls have shown that we have to rethink this school's team-sports policy."

"Ditto to that!" Belinda MacArthur hollers from her seat.

A boy from grade eight pipes up. "This school is no fun any more. The girls aren't even talking to the boys." He looks across a few rows at his girfriend. "I say we let these girls play on the boys' soccer team, and let the school get back to normal."

A round of applause fills the gym.

"Let's have our vote then, and put this matter to rest once and for all," Mr. Murray concludes. "All those in favour of allowing the girls to play on the boys' team say 'Yea.'"

Loud Yeas fill the gym. I know there's no way the boys will win this vote.

Mr. Murray pushes on. "All those opposed say 'Nay.'"

There are only a few 'Nays,' and before those few boys are even finished saying the word, the rest of the school has drowned them out with their shouts of celebration.

"We're back on the team!" I shout. "We're back on the team!"

Neena and I hug and twirl around in a tight circle. "I'm sorry I was obnoxious to you, Neena," I blurt out as we hold each other tightly. "Please forgive me," I say.

"I forgive you, I forgive you," Neena says. "You're my best friend."

"And you're mine," I say.

By then the rest of the girls make their way to us and we all embrace as we did yesterday on the soccer field. Only this time we're not soaking wet in the rain but lifted high on a thunderous wave of cheering.

When we're done, I make my way to Justin. I want to thank him personally for standing up for us.

"Thanks for everything," I say, shaking his hand. "That took a lot of guts."

Justin shrugs off my thanks. "It was the right thing to do, and we should have done it a long time ago," he says. "You should thank Neena for coming after me and some of the other boys this morning and telling us what huge sucks we were being about this whole thing."

So that's what Neena was doing this morning with all those boys, I realize now. Why couldn't I have trusted her from the very beginning? I had no reason not to.

"I'll thank her, all right," I say, smiling widely. "She's the best."

"I know," Justin says.

He really likes her, I can tell. I have to respect that.

Justin goes on. "We've got a game first thing next week against the Windsor Park Royals," he says.

"See you there," I say.

18

Same Players, New Team

Windsor Park Junior High is located halfway across the city, but still almost our entire school shows up to support the soccer team in our first game since the Soccer Showdown. The Windsor Park players and their fans, only about twenty students and a scattering of parents, are amazed as carload after busload of Corydon Junior High fans, at least two hundred of them, show up to root us on.

As Neena and I take a ball out of the equipment bag to begin our warmup passes, I look around the field and breathe in the excitement of this game. It's unbelievable. Banners hyping our team streak the sidelines. Students are chanting "Eagles! Eagles!" One parent is even blowing cavalry marches on a trumpet.

"Is this for real?" I ask Neena, sending a pass to her. Justin and Brad are warming up beside us, and Melanie and Jasmine beside them.

"Yes," Neena exclaims. "We've come a long way!"

I finger the captain's arm band around my upper arm and hope that I can prove that I deserve to wear it. Coach Borowski, with my dad's help, is preparing the goalkeepers, Natalie and Victor. The weather is fine again, sunny with a mild breeze that carries thousands of tiny pieces of fruit from the stand of elm trees behind the school sailing onto the field like so much confetti.

After Neena and I trade a few passes, Justin approaches me.

"Mind if I cut in?" he asks, smiling.

"Not at all," I say, switching places with him so that now he's passing with Neena and I'm passing with Brad.

It feels weird warming up with Brad. I mean, not only because just last week he was about as willing to accept us on the team as a student is to do detention, but also because I'm not used to his style of passing. Playing on this team with the boys as full partners, I suddenly realize, will not be a simple task. There'll be a fair amount of adjustment necessary. From both sides.

Coach Borowski calls us in then for our final instructions. "They have a tough squad. I've heard good things about them. You guys are tough, too, though, all of you. I know that. If you work together, help one another out, you can win this game. Try it for a change, you'll see how well it works."

"Control the ball," my dad adds, "and you'll control the game." I laugh; at least he didn't compare our team to some Ancient Greek army.

The referee calls two players from each team to the centre circle. Coach sends Justin and me, and we trot out together, keeping pace with each other. Already I feel like this team has pulled together.

In the centre circle, I get my first surprise of the afternoon: one of the two Windsor Park representatives is a girl, with long brown hair braided down her back and sharp green eyes.

"It's been a while since I've bumped into a girl on the soccer field," the girl says. Then she extends her hand and introduces herself. "I'm Kelly Myers."

I can't hold back a chuckle. Now the joke's really on the boys. Not only do they have to play with girls today, but they have to play against one, too. This is great!

"My name's Lizzie Lucas," I say. "Pleased to meet you."

In a few seconds, the whistle blows and the game begins.

Justin kicks the ball into play by pushing a pass to Brad. Brad dipsey-doodles around one Windsor Park defender and hustles down the left sideline. Melanie's to his immediate right and I'm hanging around the centre of the field waiting for a cross. Brad stops his charge and looks around for a free player. Melanie calls to him. I pray he passes to her. He does. I sigh with relief. Meanwhile, Melanie quickly heels the ball to me.

Nobody was expecting Melanie's backward pass and I find myself in the open. I dribble deep into the opposing end, hoping the goalkeeper will commit to coming out of the net so I can chip a shot over his head. The goalkeeper slowly veers toward me, trying to cut down my angle. Just then Brad breaks for the net. I spot him and direct a pass his way. The ball settles on Brad's foot and he taps it into the wide open net.

Corydon 1, Windsor Park 0.

"Great pass!" Brad exclaims, patting me on the back.

"Way to go!" Justin adds, high-fiving me.

Melanie and Neena hug me. From the bench, Natalie and Jasmine shout their congratulations. I love soccer. Especially when my team scores goals.

The players on the Windsor Park team, however, are no slouches, and they're not about to let in a slew of goals. Their defence tightens up, and their strikers come back with a vengeance, conducting some neat give-and-gos and several crossing passes to their centre-forward, an excellent header who must be about ten centimetres taller than I. Victor keeps us in the game with some acrobatic last-second saves, including one on Kelly Myers where he pushes her volley shot over the crossbar with the heel of his hand.

Unfortunately, Victor's heroics last only so long. Late in the first half, one of their attackers dekes around Neena and heads for the net. Tyler has a chance to stop him but he wastes a valuable second shouting an insult at Neena. That's all the opportunity needed by the Windsor Park player. He scoots by Tyler and wings a ball over Victor's head and into the net.

"Come on, Tyler," Brad snarls, "you could have stopped that play if you weren't so busy being a sourpuss."

"Lay off me!" Tyler responds.

Tyler's still being a sore loser, of course. But I'm not too worried. I know even he'll come around eventually. A person can only hold out so long.

Before the half-time break, Windsor Park manages one more goal, and our team leaves the field behind 2 to 1.

During the break, the whole team sticks together on the sideline, analysing our play. Melanie explains to Brad how she'll try to make herself open in the second half. Victor tells Natalie, who's starting the second half, how best to defend against the Windsor Park strikers, which players favour what kind of shots. Enzo and Justin ask me to teach them how to head the ball properly. I show Enzo how to throw his whole body into the header, and I try to help Justin keep his eyes open during his headers.

As we take the field for the second half, I remove the captain's arm band from my arm and hand it to Justin.

"You deserve this, too," I say.

"Thanks," he says, fitting the band around his arm.

We play our hearts out throughout the whole second half. All eleven players on the team work as one unit, bringing the ball up through our end and deep into the Windsor Park end. In ten minutes, we've tied the game up with a long shot from Justin that threads through the goalkeeper's open legs. I sit back on the grass as the goal celebrations go on and stare at the blue sky, thinking about what a big difference this game is from our first game on the boys' team.

As the game nears its end, I feel my legs tiring, but I know we still have to work hard or Windsor Park will steal the game away from us once again.

Melanie takes control then. The way she's still zipping around the field, she doesn't seem at all tired, and I find myself passing to her often, hoping she'll be able to make something happen for us. At one point, we attempt a give-and-go, but I'm too tired to pick up her forward pass. I feel bad, but she pats me on the shoulder and tells me not to worry. Coming from her, those consoling words mean a lot. This is turning out to be some game, all right.

With two minutes left in the game, Coach Borowski and my dad urge us from the sideline to press even harder. Like us, they'd really like to win today. A tie just wouldn't be the same.

We get a lucky break as one of the Windsor Park goalkeeper's clearing kicks bobbles off his foot out of bounds deep in their end. Brad, who's probably the strongest player on the team, takes the throw-in. He plants his feet firmly on the ground and arcs the ball to Justin. Justin heads the ball to Neena. Neena traps the ball with her chest and passes to Enzo. The Windsor Park defenders swarm Enzo. Somehow he pushes a pass back to the sideline, where Brad one-times it across the field to Melanie. Melanie breaks for the net. I hang back, waiting for the next move. Kelly Myers drops to her knees to tackle the ball free, but Melanie outmanoeuvres her and approaches the net, with only one defender and the goalkeeper between her and the winning goal.

Tyler is open to Melanie's left. He calls for a pass. The Windsor Park goalkeeper emerges from his net, his eyes roving back and forth between Melanie and Tyler. Again Tyler calls for the pass. Alarmed that Melanie will make the pass, the goalkeeper starts edging towards Tyler.

But Melanie keeps the ball. Like a bullet she streaks past the defender. The goaltender tries to regain position, but he's a few paces short. The whole left end of his net is wide open. Melanie takes her shot. The goalie dives. His body bangs against the dirt, raising a dust cloud, and he stretches out his arms. The ball zooms towards the net. At the last second, though, the goalkeeper's fingertips reach the ball. The ball is nudged off track and into the goalpost.

The ball ricochets off the goalpost and back into play. A mass of players converges on the net. In the confusion, I feel elbows, shoulders, legs and feet bumping against my body. Somehow I manage to keep my balance. In the next second I feel the ball against my feet. Without even stopping to look at its precise placement, I rear my leg back and take a whack. The ball soars high above all the other jabbing feet. I look up and watch as the ball sails into the Windsor Park net.

We've won!

I've never won a school soccer game before, so I go wild. Players are piling up all over me. Our bench clears to join the celebration. Everybody on the team congratulates everybody else. Like it or not, even Tyler is hugged by all us girls, and Melanie goes so far as to compliment him on serving as a decoy on her tying goal.

When the final whistle blows, the Corydon Junior High fans shriek with delight. They've got a fine team to throw their support behind now.

As a treat for winning, Coach Borowski and Dad offer to take the players out for hamburgers. One of Dad's friends owns a diner in this part of town, and he directs us there. The place is called the Olympic Diner. I remember it from the few times Dad has brought our family here to eat. Inside it looks real old-fashioned, with a wooden counter and revolving stools, and there's even a pinball machine in one corner.

Before long the atmosphere inside the diner resembles a party. I guess our team needed something like this to loosen up after all our conflicts. Justin and Neena take to the pinball machine. Natalie, Jasmine and some of the boys hold a french fry-eating contest, seeing who can stuff the most fries into their mouth at one time. Melanie, Brad, Victor and I replay the game for one another like television sportscasters, trying to wring every last ounce of pleasure out of our victory. We're having a ball.

After a while, Neena makes her way to me and pulls me aside. Her face is flushed and her sapphire eyes are sparkling.

"Justin just asked me to the year-end dance!" she gushes.

"Your idea to play soccer and win friends sure payed off," I offer.

"With your help, Lizzie."

Neena always knows exactly what to say to make me feel good.

"I'm worried, though," Neena goes on. "I mean, are my parents even going to let me go to the dance?"

"We'll figure something out," I say.

"We always do, don't we?"

"You can say that again."

All of a sudden I'm feeling like Neena and I are best friends again. I don't ever want that feeling to go away again.

"Can I tell you something personal?" I ask Neena. I'm grinning.

"Anything." Neena's eyes pop wide.

"I think I've got a crush on Enzo Milano."

"No way!" Neena smiles and rubs her hands together fiendishly. "We'll double date to the dance, and we can wear matching outfits, and ..."

"Hold on," I say, "I haven't even asked him out yet."

"So what are you waiting for?"

"I don't know." I turn my eyes away from Neena. "I guess I'm too shy."

"Lizzie Lucas, shy? You've got to be kidding!"

"I have kind of made a reputation for myself as something of a big mouth lately, haven't I?"

"You bet!"

We both laugh.

"Still, how do I do it? I mean, what if he says no? What if he already has a date? I mean, how do I even know if he likes me?"

"Believe me, it's not easy," Neena replies, biting the bottom of her lip and shaking her head. "Look at what I went through with Justin."

"And boys don't make it any easier for you, do they?" I observe.

Neena and I put our arms over each other's shoulders.

"It's not easy being a woman," Neena says then.

"I agree," I say, and then we hug tightly.